OTHER YEARLING BOOKS YOU WILL ENJOY:

THE BLOOD-AND-THUNDER ADVENTURE ON
HURRICANE PEAK, *Margaret Mahy*
THE HAUNTING, *Margaret Mahy*
NONSTOP NONSENSE, *Margaret Mahy*
THE WITCH HERSELF, *Phyllis Reynolds Naylor*
WITCH WATER, *Phyllis Reynolds Naylor*
WITCH'S SISTER, *Phyllis Reynolds Naylor*
THE DOOR IN THE WALL, *Marguerite de Angeli*
THE LION IN THE BOX, *Marguerite de Angeli*
FIVE-FINGER DISCOUNT, *Barthe DeClements*
MONKEY SEE. MONKEY DO., *Barthe DeClements*

YEARLING BOOKS/YOUNG YEARLINGS/YEARLING CLASSICS
are designed especially to entertain and enlighten
young people. Patricia Reilly Giff, consultant to this
series, received her bachelor's degree from Marymount
College and a master's degree in history from St. John's
University. She holds a Professional Diploma in Reading and a Doctorate of Humane Letters from Hofstra
University. She was a teacher and reading consultant
for many years, and is the author of numerous books for
young readers.

For a complete listing of all Yearling titles,
write to Dell Readers Service,
P.O. Box 1045, South Holland, IL 60473.

MARGARET MAHY

The Door in the Air

and Other Stories

Illustrated by

Diana Catchpole.

A Yearling Book

To the other children of the other bridge builder—
Helen, Patricia, Frank, and Cecily

Published by
Dell Publishing
a division of
Bantam Doubleday Dell Publishing Group, Inc.
666 Fifth Avenue
New York, New York 10103

ISBN: 0-440-40774-5

Reprinted by arrangement with Delacorte Press

Printed in the United States of America

April 1993

10 9 8 7 6 5 4 3 2 1

CWO

Contents

The Door in the Air   1

The Two Sisters   13

The Bridge Builder   21

A Work of Art   36

The Wind Between the Stars   50

Perdita and Maddy   59

The House of Coloured Windows   69

The Hookywalker Dancers   78

The Magician in the Tower   90

The Door in the Air

The girl on the trapeze was called Aquilina, which means 'Little Eagle'.

When she was born her mother had tossed her lightly over to her father, and her father, the trapeze master of the famous acrobat circus, caught the new baby and then held her up high, offering her back to the air.

"Ah, my little eagle!" he said. "You shall be the trapeze queen of the world, beginning from now. Never, never will you set foot on common ground." He hung her cradle, shaped like a new moon, from the trapeze (though he did put the landing net under it for safety).

Never had anyone been so much a child of the air. By the time she was five, Aquilina leaned against the ropes of her trapeze as other people lean against the frames of their own back doors. She felt that this trapeze — its two ropes and its crossbar — really was a door — her door, with the acrobat circus in front of it and, behind it, the true kingdom

1

of the air. She felt she was balanced between the two. Aquilina was careful never to dive backwards from the trapeze. She always dived *forwards*, crying out in a bird voice as she flung herself out into the air of the circus tent. All watchers gasped, not because they thought she would fall, but because they thought she just might fly. However, in that second between either flying or falling, Aquilina's father would always sweep in on his trapeze and pick her out of the air as delicately as if he were picking a rose with thorns. No one dared guess what would happen if he missed.

One day, the acrobat circus arrived in a city of stone towers, clocks and narrow streets, and put up their famous green tents on the edge of the beautiful but dangerous wood called Riddle Chase. No man or woman with any sense ever went into Riddle Chase, for its tracks were all tricks. People who tried to follow the paths wandered in circles all night and emerged quite different from the way they had been before. Some began to write poetry, but several poets gave up poetry altogether and became plumbers.

The acrobat circus was commanded to perform for the prince of the city, as well as for his mother and her ladies-in-waiting. No one else was allowed to attend that night. Some people said that the queen didn't want people looking at the prince too closely. After all, when he was very small, his nurse had once gone to sleep in the sun and he had wandered out through a forgotten gate in the castle wall. Down through fields he had walked where butterflies fluttered among the grassheads, down still further into Riddle Chase. There, he had wandered in circles all night and come out changed, for being a prince could not protect

2

him from the enchanted wood. However, no one knew just how he had been changed. It was nothing that showed, and the queen would not discuss it. His nurse said he talked about a golden net, travellers with their hair blowing out behind them, a door in the sky, and a gatekeeper like a thundercloud who asked him for a ticket. Mind you, who could believe what a nurse who went to sleep in the sun had to say about anything?

Just before her father turned the spotlights on, Aquilina looked down and saw the prince far, far below her, sitting on a little velvet chair. He must have felt her looking at him, because he suddenly looked up at her. He was about five, her own age, a gentle boy, with straight fair hair growing long like a unicorn's mane. She could not see the colour of his eyes, but she could see something else in the strange light of the acrobat circus. There was a star on his forehead just below the rim of his crown. As for the prince, when he saw Aquilina up there on the highest trapeze, dressed in silver tights painted with flashes of lightning, staring out of the black thundercloud of her hair, he laughed and waved as if she were an old friend. But then the spotlights came on. Aquilina, drenched in gold, cried out, dived forwards, swooping down towards him. The moment came. All nature held its breath. Then her father, with brilliant timing, swung over, pulling her back out of the arms of the air.

Aquilina would have liked to see the prince again and look more closely at the star, grown into the very skin of his forehead. But the acrobat circus was always moving on. The world went in a circle round the sun and the circus went in a circle round the world, and Aquilina, who was always up above the world on her trapeze, could see everything that was going on. Every now and then, something behind the door which the trapeze made in the air tapped her on the shoulder, and whispered in her ear. *Look! Let go! Leap out!* it seemed to say. *Leap to the place where no one will gather you back out of the air.* But there was always so much going on in front of her that Aquilina never looked over her shoulder. She never dived off backwards.

The famous acrobat circus went through hot lands and cold lands, through forests and over stormy seas. They performed for kings and farmers, bellringers, television announcers and pirates. They performed for anyone who crossed the ticket-seller's palm with silver and bought a ticket — and at last one day they came into a city full of narrow streets and chiming clocks which Aquilina recognized at once.

"Haven't we been here before?" she asked her father.

"Five years ago," he shouted up to her. "But I don't think we'll see the prince again. People say he has grown too strange to be looked at. He scarcely ever comes out of his castle, and when he does he wears a big hat with a beekeeper's veil. The queen pretends it's because he is fond of beekeeping, but no one believes her."

However, as it happened, the queen had decided it was time for people to see that the prince was, at least, alive and well, so she brought him to the circus a few nights later. People waved as he rode through the streets, but no one was able to look at him closely for, sure enough, he was wearing a beekeeper's veil. Only two tickets were sold for this entire performance, though of course they were for the very best seats. Even the ladies-in-waiting were left at home this time.

Standing on the crossbar of her trapeze, Aquilina looked

down just before the spotlights were turned on, and saw the prince taking off his hat. Once again she saw his long fair mane, but this time his face was dappled with silver stars, and it even seemed that the stars were being joined together by a web of golden threads. When he saw her looking down he gave her a secret wave and, due to some trick of the light, she saw that, although his hair was fair, his eyes looking out through the web of stars were very clear and dark. They were the colour she thought she might see if ever she bothered to look over her shoulder, back between the ropes of the trapeze. But then the spotlights came on, and everything beyond the rim of light vanished. So she gave her strange cry and flung herself forwards from the bar of her trapeze.

As she swooped down towards the prince she heard the queen gasp. The prince, though, laughed aloud at the wonder of seeing a girl about to fly like a bird. But Aquilina's father swung over and snatched her out of the air. He snatched at her very quickly these days, because he was beginning to be afraid that his little eagle, whom he had offered so willingly to the air, might somehow fly away from him.

The next day the circus went on its way around the world once more – over the desert, over the sea, through a country with no roads, only thousands of rivers. Aquilina rode high on her trapeze which was carried by truck when it wasn't carried by barge. The acrobat circus spread out in front of her, and she noticed her father and mother looking up at her like people who aren't quite sure what they are seeing.

For these days, though Aquilina never looked behind her, her head was full of pictures of the kingdom of the air, held by a net of gold, while the stars sang to one another in golden voices. Aquilina thought she saw suns touching fingers of light, and comets passing like rare visitors, their hair blown out behind them by the power of sunlight falling on it. Some stars clustered like swarming bees, and when suns were eclipsed, huge shadows rushed past. Coronas, like folds of luminous silk, shook themselves out in that clear darkness – the exact colour of the eyes of the prince. Behind the trapeze, she guessed, she would be able to fly freely, and no one would be able to pull her out of the air. She wondered whether she might need a map to find her way from star to star. But, for the moment, the circus was too entertaining for Aquilina to want to turn her back on it.

One day Aquilina heard clocks chiming and, looking down from her trapeze, saw narrow streets and stone towers, and the trees of a mysterious forest. The circus went through town and stopped in the usual place, right on the edge of Riddle Chase.

"Haven't we been here before?" she asked.

"Five years ago," said her father, "but now the prince has changed so much that he isn't allowed out. The queen has had a high wall built by robots in the middle of that wood, and he has to live behind the wall, guarded by robot-guards who are not likely to be changed by anything the forest tells them."

"That's a pity. He had such a nice laugh," said Aquilina sadly.

"Never mind!" said Aquilina's father. "The queen herself is coming to see us tomorrow night, so we will have a royal command performance after all."

Late the following afternoon, Aquilina left the circus for

the first time in her life. She left her trapezes, but she didn't come down to the ground. Instead, she leaped for the topmost branches of Riddle Chase, travelling by trees that stayed true rather than by tracks that turned out to be tricks. Off she went in her silver tights, painted all over with strokes of lightning, her hair streaming behind her like a thundercloud as she swung up, down and along the green ladders of the forest. At last she saw the great wall, looming up so high before her that only the tallest trees could look over the top of it. Aquilina made a springboard of the last branch, landed on the top of the wall, and looked over.

The wall had been built around the very heart of the forest. The space behind it was full of trees, although some had been cut down by the robots, leaving a wide gap between the heart of the forest and the wall. The trees grew very thickly, but there, running between them like a wild man, was the prisoner, the prince himself. He was thin, and so ragged that he was almost naked, but his bare skin burned with stars held together with golden threads. He had become a map of the space behind the trapeze, and he was running, running for ever inside the wall, trying to find the place his skin was describing. His hair grew down his neck, even down his spine, and flew out behind him like the tail of a comet. As he ran he cried aloud, "Riddle Chase! Riddle Chase!" over and over again.

"Prince!" Aquilina called down to him. "I know how you can come to the end of *your* Riddle Chase."

He stopped running and turned his starry face up to hers. Then he laughed.

"It's the gatekeeper," he called. "You've certainly taken your time getting here."

"Climb the big tree there," she said to him, but he was already beginning to climb from branch to branch, up and up until his dark, clear eyes were level with her own.

"Jump!" she called.

It was too far from the tree to the wall, but the prince did not hesitate. He flung himself forward as if he might fly rather than fall. Aquilina, meeting him half way, picked him out of the air in the very second when he was poised between sky and earth. There was a shout from below. The robot-guards had seen them. As Aquilina and the prince vanished among the leaves, mechanical dogs with teeth of iron were let loose, and steel traps, triggered by computer, gaped under the ferns of the forest floor. The guards, in their curious armour, searched in hollows and holes while the prince and Aquilina swung side by side above, pursued through Riddle Chase. But the air knew Aquilina was its true child, and it held both of them up, opening and closing around them like silk.

Of course, in Riddle Chase the tracks were tricks, and bent round and swallowed themselves. After a while the robots were running in circles. Only the one with the best program managed to solve most of the tricks, and when even he could not, he simply left the track and followed the starry shimmer that was the prince in the tops of the trees.

Inside the circus tent all was confusion, for Aquilina was nowhere to be found. The acrobats built up toppling castles from their own bodies, the jugglers juggled apples and oranges, chairs and tennis rackets and flaming torches, and Aquilina's parents swung through the air like spider

9

monkeys. But all the performers in the acrobat circus were wondering just what the queen would say when she found there would be no Aquilina. There she sat in her velvet chair with her nephew beside her. He had no stars on him, for he had never escaped into Riddle Chase, had never been changed, or been made more than himself. And because there was nothing to hide this time, everyone in the town had bought tickets and the tent was full of cheering and clapping.

Just as the acrobats were wondering what would happen next, down through one of the flaps of the tent, open to the summer night, came Aquilina herself, landing light as a leaf on the crossbar of her father's trapeze. Everyone shouted and stood up in surprise, for they all had a perfect view of her, even though the spotlights were not turned on. She was flooded in the light of a thousand stars because, tumbling after her, came a young man with a pale mane, and the light came out of him. He would have fallen past her like a shooting star, but Aquilina swung down after him and caught his ankles, just in time.

Into the tent rushed the best of the robot-guards, stopping under the trapeze to bleep crossly to itself. Then it extended a ladder from its own head and began to climb up itself, with terrible screeching, for it was very difficult, even for a well-programmed robot, to do this. But just as it seemed it might get its mechanical hands on the prince, Aquilina swung him up and across to her special trapeze, and then followed him over. They stood together in the doorway of the air, one leaning on one rope, one leaning on the other. And now, beyond them, framed in the ropes of the trapeze, everyone could see a slot of darkness even in the middle of the circus light, and swarming stars, the

11

suns touching fingers of light, and comets with their tails streaming behind them.

"I think that must be the *star* circus. You'll need a ticket to get in," said Aquilina. "Cross my palm with silver." She held out her hand, and the prince took it and kissed her palm. Where he kissed it a silver star formed. "Oh yes, that'll do," Aquilina said, laughing. The prince stepped through into the space, which knew exactly who he was, and held him safely.

"Aren't you coming too?" he asked.

"Oh yes, I will, now I have a good map," Aquilina replied. She waved to the queen, and to her parents. Her father swung towards her on his trapeze hoping to catch her before it was too late, but she gave a cry like a bird, dived backwards for the very first time, and vanished from sight. The door in the air closed at once. The circus light went right between the ropes of the trapeze once more, for the little eagle had flown away, taking the map of the stars with her. There was nothing anyone could do about it. The very next day the acrobat circus folded its tents and set off on its travels around the world again, taking with it its empty trapeze – in case Aquilina might some day return.

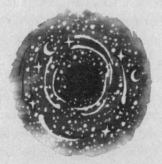

The Two Sisters

A man and his wife once had twin daughters. The two babies lying in their cradle looked exactly alike. The only difference was that one lay on the left-hand side of the cradle and one on the right, and once that was changed there was nobody who could tell one from the other. The parents looked at their children and they both worried. But they worried about different things.

The man looked at the babies and thought, How shall I manage? As these children grow older they'll eat more and more and they'll have to have shoes and dresses. What a terrible responsibility it is being a father. Whereas his wife thought, How shall I tell them apart? How will I give them names and teach them to come when they're called? How will I prevent these two darling babies from getting mixed up with each other? How difficult it is to be a mother.

That very night the man had a dream. He dreamed that he opened his eyes and there, standing beside him, was a tall, dark-haired woman in black, with eyes like dark holes in her pale face. She smiled at him so strangely that he was too terrified to speak, but it did not matter for she spoke to him.

"You have two daughters," she said, "and you are worried about how to care for them. Give me one to be my servant and you shall never want for food or drink or shelter. You shall have all manner of left-handed luck and live in prosperity until the end of your days."

In his dream the man nodded, for he was still too frightened to speak. Then the dark woman, still smiling her ominous smile, took a pin from the bosom of her black dress and pricked her left forefinger. She touched the baby that lay on the left-hand side of the cradle, leaving a tiny spot of blood on the child's left eyelid.

"Sleep left, dream, sinister,

Darkness be your king and minister," said the dark woman, and vanished as a shadow vanishes when the candle is blown out and all shadows become part of the vast shadow of night.

Meanwhile, the man's wife was dreaming too. She dreamed that she opened her eyes and saw beside her bed a woman bright as day, with summer-gold hair and summer-blue eyes, a golden skin, and a golden belt around her waist. She smiled a smile so clear and sunny that the woman was struck dumb by its bright enchantment, but it did not matter because the bright lady spoke to her instead.

"You have new twin daughters. And you are worried about how you will tell one child from another. Give me your right-hand daughter to be my servant and I will be her good guardian. As for you — you will have all kinds

14

of right-handed luck, and you will always be able to tell one child from the other."

The mother still could not speak but she could smile, and in the dream she smiled and nodded. The golden lady laughed and, pricking her right forefinger on the thorn of a red rose, she pressed the bead of blood against the baby's right eyelid and said,

"Dream, dexter, sleep right,
You shall be the child of light."

Then the lady vanished and the woman slept on without dreaming again.

In the morning, when she and her husband awoke, they kissed each other and fussed over their beautiful babies, but neither one of them told the other of their dreams and their promises. After all, each of them thought, there are some bargains best not told even to those we love.

The two children were called Jennifer and Jessica and though no one else could tell them apart to begin with, from the very first their mother could always recognize Jennifer. Later, when their hair grew, and their eyes turned from baby-blue to their true colours, everyone could tell them apart. For Jennifer had one blue eye and one green, and Jessica had one green eye and one as black as night. When they grew older still other differences showed. For Jennifer looked at the world and laughed and sang, while Jessica rested her chin in her hands and stared gravely and darkly. She never laughed, but if she smiled, as she sometimes did, it was like a shadow creeping over the face of the moon – taking light rather than giving it. People loved Jennifer easily, but Jessica – even though she did no harm – frightened them, for her black eye seemed to look through them right to their hearts and read there the secrets

15

that they tried to keep hidden from the world.

"Our parents love one another and they love us," Jennifer sang. "We are the luckiest children in the world."

"Our parents deceive one another, and gave us away to the powers of light and darkness on the very night we were born," sighed Jessica.

"We have each other," Jennifer said.

"For a while," said Jessica, "but nothing lasts for ever."

As they grew older it became more and more easy to tell them apart, for Jennifer's brown hair came to have golden lights in it and her green eye became bluer, while Jessica's brown hair grew darker and darker and her green eye grew darker, too. Jennifer grew rosy and golden, but Jessica grew paler and paler, like a child of the moon.

"No one would think they were sisters, let alone twins," said their mother. "It's very strange. Jessica does things crookedly because she uses her left hand. She's a contrary child, and though she's my own daughter sometimes she seems like a stranger to me," and she began to say that Jennifer was her child, but that Jessica was her father's.

One day the mother of the two girls became angry with her husband, over some small thing. Because she was cross she said to him,

"Look how my daughter, Jennifer, sings and laughs, while your daughter, Jessica, sits silent and never ever has a song on her lips. My daughter has all the songs and yours has none."

"Of course she has songs too," the father said. "You sing songs, don't you, Jessica?"

"I know one song," Jessica said, "but nobody should ask to hear it. It's a song from the left-hand side of the night and it is very beautiful, but it can only be heard once."

Her father was now very curious. When Jessica went down into the garden to gather apples, he came after her and said, "I am your father, Jessica, and I think you should let me hear your song. Don't you hear how your mother teases us because you are silent? If you love me, sing me your song."

"Because I love you I don't want to sing it to you," Jessica said. "My song is only heard once, remember, and after my song, there are no other songs ever again."

"Jessica," said her father. "I am your father and I have clothed you and fed you for many years. You owe me something. I command you to sing me your song."

"Very well," Jessica whispered, "but it is against my will."

Standing under the apple tree she sang her song. The apples shrank on the branches, the leaves fell, the tree died and her father fell to the ground and died, too. Jessica shed tears like black diamonds, stroked his hair and closed his eyes. Then she went sadly up to the house to tell her mother and Jennifer.

Years went by. The twins' mother grew old and her two daughters cared for her. Jennifer was still her favourite, bringing her gifts of flowers, gifts of fruit, gifts of wild honey, nuts and strawberries, singing in and out of the house like some golden bird.

"Why don't you bring me presents?" the mother once asked Jessica, who moved silently around the house, darkening the rooms as she passed through them. "I've been a good mother to you and you have grown into a silent, sulky girl who gives nothing."

"I have only one gift to give," Jessica replied, "and I will give it to you when you ask for it. For you will ask for it one day and then I shall give it to you with a full heart." The mother grew silent and did not speak to Jessica again about gifts.

Time passed and though neither Jennifer nor Jessica appeared to grow older, their mother did. One day she pushed aside the roses Jennifer brought her and said, "They no longer smell sweet." And a day or two later she refused to take a spoonful of Jennifer's honey on her bread. "It has no taste left," she sighed. And, later still, she would not eat the wild strawberries Jennifer brought her, because she said they had no flavour.

"Jennifer, why do you laugh and sing," she complained, "when I am tired and I ache all over, and can scarcely see you any more?"

"I laugh and sing because you made me a servant of the lady of light," Jennifer replied. "Remember that old bargain? I have given you many gifts and sung you many songs, and they are all the gifts and songs from the right-handed side of the world. I have nothing else to give you."

The mother was silent for a moment and then she sighed and said,

"Is Jessica there?"

"I've always been here," said Jessica, "and I can tell that now you want to hear my song and take the one gift I have to give. And after that, Jennifer and I will set out on our travels, servants no longer, but mistresses of light and darkness. Still, Mother, that was a strange bargain that you and our father made, for all people should be dappled, shadows and light both, and not wholly one thing or the other. I have never known how to laugh, and Jennifer cannot cry, whereas all true men and women can do both things."

"Forgive me," said the mother.

"You are forgiven," said Jennifer.

"Forgiven," echoed Jessica.

Then Jessica sang her beautiful, terrible song which was her gift, and the mother died quietly, smiling peacefully.

For the first time in their lives the two sisters were alone. They tidied the house and locked the door. Then they wandered together down the road with their arms around each other's waists, talking of their childhood together and the times they had shared, their many birthdays, their different views of the world. The sun was setting in the west and the moon, still blue with daylight, was rising in the east. At last, they came to a crossroads where one road ran west into the last of the day's sunlight, and another into a shadowy valley where darkness was already gathering.

"Here we must go our separate ways," Jennifer said. "We have sung our songs and given our gifts and now we must enter into our true power."

"Indeed, this is where we begin," Jessica agreed. "Everything up until now has been preparation. Oh, Jennifer, both your eyes are quite, quite blue."

"Yours are as black as night," said Jennifer. "Our long childhood is over. If I could be sorry I would cry at leaving you, but it is not in my power to grieve."

Then she walked into the sunlight and before she was out of sight Jessica heard her laugh and sing and saw her stoop to gather wild flowers.

"Nothing lasts for ever," said Jessica. "Goodbye, Jennifer!" and she smiled her smile that took light out of the air and gave nothing back. Then, like a true princess of darkness, she turned and walked into the shadowy valley where she soon became part of the night.

The Bridge Builder

My father was a bridge builder. That was his business — crossing chasms, joining one side of the river with the other.

When I was small, bridges brought us bread and books, Christmas crackers and coloured pencils — one-span bridges over creeks, two-span bridges over streams, three-span bridges over wide rivers. Bridges sprang from my father's dreams threading roads together — girder bridges, arched bridges, suspension bridges, bridges of wood, bridges of iron or concrete. Like a sort of hero, my father would drive piles and piers through sand and mud to the rocky bones of the world. His bridges became visible parts of the world's hidden skeleton. When we went out on picnics it was along roads held together by my father's works. As we crossed rivers and ravines we heard each bridge singing in its own private language. We could hear the melody, but my father was the only one who understood the words.

There were three of us when I was small: Philippa, the oldest, Simon in the middle, and me, Merlin, the youngest, the one with the magician's name. We played where bridges were being born, running around piles of sand and shingle, bags of cement and bars of reinforced steel. Concrete mixers would turn, winches would wind, piles would be driven and decking cast. Slowly, as we watched and played, a bridge would appear and people could cross over.

For years my father built bridges where people said they wanted them, while his children stretched up and out in three different directions. Philippa became a doctor and Simon an electrical engineer, but I became a traveller, following the roads of the world and crossing the world's bridges as I came to them.

My father, however, remained a bridge builder. When my mother died and we children were grown up and gone, and there was no more need for balloons and books or Christmas crackers and coloured pencils, his stored powers were set free and he began to build the bridges he saw in his dreams.

The first of his new bridges had remarkable handrails of black iron lace. But this was not enough for my father. He collected a hundred orb-web spiders and set them loose in the crevices and curlicues of the iron. Within the lace of the bridge, these spiders spun their own lace, and after a night of rain or dew the whole bridge glittered black and silver, spirals within spirals, an intricate piece of jewellery arching over a wide, stony stream.

People were enchanted with the unexpectedness of it. Now, as they crossed over, they became part of a work of art. But the same people certainly thought my father

strange when he built another bridge of horsehair and vines so that rabbits, and even mice, could cross the river with dry feet and tails. He's gone all funny, they said, turning their mouths down. However, my father had only just begun. He made two bridges with gardens built into them which soon became so overgrown with roses, wisteria, bougainvillea and other beautiful climbing plants that they looked as if they had been made entirely of flowers.

Over a river that wound through a grove of silver birch trees he wove a bridge of golden wires, a great cage filled with brilliant, singing birds; and in a dull, tired town he made an aquarium bridge whose glass balustrades and parapets were streaked scarlet and gold by the fish that darted inside them. People began to go out of their way to cross my father's bridges.

Building surprising bridges was one thing, but soon my father took it into his head to build bridges in unexpected places. He gave up building them where people were known to be going and built them where people might happen to find themselves. Somewhere, far from any road, sliding through brush and ferns to reach a remote stretch of river, you might find one of my father's bridges: perhaps a strong one built to last a thousand years, perhaps a frail one made of bamboo canes, peacock feathers and violin strings. A bridge like this would soon fall to pieces sending its peacock feathers down the river like messages, sounding a single twangling note among the listening hills. Mystery became a part of crossing over by my father's bridges.

In some ways it seemed as if his ideas about what a bridge should be were changing. His next bridge, made of silver thread and mother of pearl, was only to be crossed at midnight on a moonlight night. So, crossing over changed, too. Those who crossed over from one bank to another on this bridge, crossed also from one day to another, crossing time as well as the spaces under the piers. It was his first time-bridge, but later there was to be another, a bridge set with clocks chiming perpetually the hours and half hours in other parts of the world. And in all the world this was the only bridge that needed to be wound up with a master key every eight days.

Wherever my father saw a promising space he thought of ways in which it could be crossed, and yet for all that he loved spaces. In the city he climbed like a spider, stringing blue suspension bridges between skyscrapers and tower blocks — air bridges, he called them. Looking up at them from the street they became invisible. When crossing over on them, you felt you were suspended in nothing, or were maybe set in crystal, a true inhabitant of the sky. Lying down, looking through the blue web that held you, you could see the world turning below. But if you chose to lie on your back and look up as far as you could look, and then a bit farther still, on and on, higher and higher, your eyes would travel through the troposphere and the tropopause, the stratosphere and the stratopause, the mesophere and the mesopause, the Heaviside layer, the ionosphere and the Appleton layer, not to mention the Van Allen belts. From my father's blue suspension bridges all the architecture of the air would open up to you.

However, not many people bothered to stare upwards like that. Only the true travellers were fascinated to realize that the space they carelessly passed through was not empty, but crowded with its own invisible constructions.

"Who wants a bridge like that, anyway?" some people asked sourly.

"Anyone. Someone!" my father answered. "There are no rules for crossing over."

But a lot of people disagreed with this idea of my father's. Such people thought bridges were designed specially for cars, mere pieces of road stuck up on legs of iron or concrete, whereas my father thought bridges were the connections that would hold everything together. Bridges gone, perhaps the whole world would fall apart, like a quartered orange. The journey on the left bank of the river (according to my father) was quite different from the journey on the right. The man on the right bank of the ravine — was he truly the same man when he crossed on to the left? My father thought he might not be, and his bridges seemed like the steps of a dance which would enable the man with a bit of left-hand spin on him to spin in the opposite direction. This world (my father thought) was playing a great game called "Change", and his part in the game was called "crossing over".

It was upsetting for those people who wanted to stick to the road to know that some people used my father's hidden bridges. They wanted everyone to cross by exactly the same bridges that *they* used, and they hated the thought that, somewhere over the river they were crossing, there might be another strange and lovely bridge they were unaware of.

However, no one could cross all my father's bridges. No one can cross over in every way. Some people became angry when they realized this and, because they could not cross over on every bridge there was, they started insisting that there should be no more bridge building. Some of these people were very powerful — so powerful, indeed, that they passed laws forbidding my father to build any bridge unless ordered to do so by a government or by some county council. They might as well have passed a law saying that the tide was only allowed to come in and out by government decree, because by now my father's bridge building had become a force beyond the rule of law. He built another bridge, a secret one, which was not discovered until he had finished it, this time over a volcano. Its abutments were carved out of old lava and, along its side, great harps, instead of handrails, cast strange, striped shadows on the decking. Men, women and children who crossed over could look down into the glowing heart of the volcano, could watch it simmer and seethe and smoulder. And when the winds blew, or when the great fumes of hot air billowed up like dragon's breath, the harps played fiery music with no regard to harmony. This bridge gave the volcano a voice. It spoke an incandescent language, making the night echo with inexplicable songs and poetry.

"The bridge will melt when the volcano erupts," people said to each other, alarmed and fascinated by these anthems of fire.

"But none of my bridges are intended to last for ever," my father muttered to himself, loading his derrick and winch on to the back of his truck and driving off in another direction. It was just as well he kept on the move. Powerful enemies pursued him.

"Bridges are merely bits of the road with special problems," they told one another, and sent soldiers out to trap my father, to arrest him, to put an end to his bridge building. Of course, they couldn't catch him. They would think they had him cornered and, behold, he would build a bridge and escape — a bridge that collapsed behind him as if it had been made of playing cards, or a bridge that unexpectedly turned into a boat, carrying his astonished pursuers away down some swift river.

Just about then, as it happened, my travelling took me on my first circle around the world, and I wound up back where I had started from. My brother, the electrical engineer, and my sister, the doctor, came to see me camping under a bridge that my father had built when I was only three years old.

"Perhaps you can do something about him," Philippa cried. "He won't listen to us."

"Don't you care?" asked Simon. "It's a real embarrassment. It's time he was stopped before he brings terrible trouble upon himself."

They looked at me — shaggy and silent, with almost nothing to say to them — in amazement. I gave them the only answer I could.

"What is there for a bridge builder to build, if he isn't allowed to build bridges?" I asked them. Dust from the world's roads made my voice husky, even in my own ears.

"He can be a retired bridge builder," Simon replied. "But I can see that you're going to waste time asking riddles. You don't care that your old father is involved in illegal bridge-building." And he went away. He had forgotten the weekend picnics in the sunshine, and the derrick, high as a ladder, leading to the stars.

"And what have you become, Merlin?" Philippa asked me. "What are you now, after all your journeys?"

"I'm a traveller as I always have been," I replied.

"You are a vagabond," she answered scornfully. "A

28

vagabond with a magician's name, but no magic!"

Then she went away, too, in her expensive car. I did not tell her, but I did have a little bit of magic — a single magical word, half-learned, half-invented. I could see that my father might need help, even a vagabond's help, even the help of a single magic word. I set off to find him.

It was easy for me, a seasoned traveller, to fall in with my father. I just walked along, until I came to a river that sang his name, and then I followed that river up over slippery stones and waterfalls, through bright green tangles of cress and monkey musk. Sure enough, there was my father building a bridge by bending two tall trees over the water and plaiting the branches into steps. This bridge would, in time, grow leafy handrails filled with birds' nests, a crossing place for deer and possums.

"Hello!" said my father. "Hello, Merlin. I've just boiled the billy. Care for a cup of tea?"

"Love one!" I said. "There's nothing quite like a cup of billy-tea." So we sat down in a patch of sunlight and drank our tea.

"They're catching up with me, you know," my father said sadly. "There are police and soldiers looking all the time. Helicopters, too! I can go on escaping, of course, but I'm not sure if I can be bothered. I'm getting pretty bored with it all. Besides," he went on, lowering his voice as if the green shadows might overhear him, "I'm not sure that building bridges is enough any longer. I feel I must become more involved, to cross over myself in some way. But how does a bridge builder learn to cross over when he's on both sides of the river to begin with?"

"I might be able to help," I said.

My father looked up from under the brim of his working

hat. He was a weatherbeaten man, fingernails cracked by many years of bridge building. Sitting there, a cup of billy-tea between his hands, he looked like a tree, he looked like a rock. There was no moss on him, but he looked mossy for all that. He was as lined and wrinkled as if a map of all his journeys, backwards and forwards, were inscribed on his face, with crosses for all the bridges he had built.

"I'm not sure you can," he answered. "I must be *more* of a bridge builder not *less* of one, if you understand me."

"Choosy, aren't you?" I said, smiling, and he smiled back.

"I suppose you think you know what I'd like most," he went on.

"I think I do!" I replied. "I've crossed a lot of bridges myself one way and another, because I'm a travelling man, and I've learned a lot on the banks of many rivers."

"And you've a magical name," my father reminded me eagerly. "I said, when you were born, this one is going to be the magician of the family!"

"I'm not a magician," I replied, "but there *is* one word I know ... a word of release and remaking. It allows things to become their true selves." My father was silent for a moment, nodding slowly, eyes gleaming under wrinkled lids.

"Don't you think things are really what they seem to be?" he asked me.

"I think people are all, more or less, creatures of two sides with a chasm in between, so to speak. My magic word merely closes the chasm."

"A big job for one word," said my father.

"Well, it's a very good word," I said. I didn't tell him I

had invented half of it myself. "It's a sort of bridge," I told him.

All the time we talked, we had felt the movement of men, not very close, not very far, as the forest carried news of my father's pursuers. Now we heard a sudden sharp cry – and another – and another. Men shouted in desperate voices.

"It's the soldiers," my father said, leaping to his feet. "They've been hunting me all day, though the forest is on my side and hides me away. But something's happened. We'd better go and check what's going on. I don't want them to come to harm because of me and my bridge-building habits."

We scrambled upstream until the river suddenly started to run more swiftly, narrow and deep. The opposite bank rose up sharply, red with crumbling, rotten rock, green with mosses and pockets of fern. My father struggled to keep up with me. He was old, and besides, he was a bridge builder, not a traveller. Closing my eyes for a moment against the distractions around me, I brought the magic word out of my mind and on to the tip of my tongue – and then I left it unspoken.

The soldiers were on the opposite bank. They had tried to climb down the cliff on rotten rock but it had broken away at their very toes and there they were, marooned on a crumbling ledge – three of them – weighted down with guns, ammunition belts and other military paraphernalia. Two of the soldiers were very young, and all three of them were afraid, faces pale, reflecting the green leaves greenly.

Below them the rocks rose out of the water. Just at this point the river became a dragon's mouth, full of black teeth, hissing and roaring, sending up a faint smoke of silver spray.

It was obvious that the soldiers needed a bridge.

My father stared at them, and they stared at him like men confounded. But he was a bridge-builder before he was anybody's friend or enemy, before he was anybody's father.

"That word?" he asked me. "You have it there?"

I nodded. I dared not speak, or the word would be said too soon.

"When I step into the water, say it then, Merlin!"

I waited and my father smiled at me, shy and proud and mischievous all at once. He looked up once at the sky, pale blue and far, and then he stepped, one foot on land, one in the water, towards the opposite bank. I spoke the word.

My father changed before my eyes. He became a bridge as he had known he would. As for the word – it whispered over the restless surface of the river and rang lightly on the red, rotten rock. But my father had taken its magic out of it. No one else was altered.

The curious thing was that my father, who had made so many strange and beautiful bridges, was a very ordinary-looking bridge himself – a single-span bridge built of stone over an arch of stone, springing upwards at an odd angle, vanishing into the cliff at the very feet of the terrified soldiers. He looked as if he had always been there, as if he would be there for ever, silver moss on his handrails, on his abutments, even on his deck. Certainly he was the quietest bridge I had ever crossed as I went over to help the soldiers down. There was no way forward through the cliff. Still, perhaps the job of some rare bridges is to cross over only briefly and then bring us back to the place we started from.

We came back together, the three soldiers and I, and I'm sure we were all different men on the right bank from the men we had been on the left.

Our feet made no sound on the silver moss.

"They can say what they like about that old man," cried the older soldier all of a sudden, "but I was never so pleased to see a bridge in all my life. It just shows there are good reasons for having bridges in unexpected places."

Together we scrambled downstream, and at last, back on to the road.

"But who's going to build the bridges now, then?" asked one of the young soldiers. "Look! You were with him. Are you a bridge-builder, too?"

They knew now. They knew that unexpected bridges would be needed.

But someone else will have to build them. I am not a bridge-builder. I am a traveller. I set out travelling, after that, crossing, one by one, all the bridges my father had built ... the picnic-bridges of childhood, the wooden ones, the steel ones, the stone and the concrete. I crossed the blue bridges of the air and those that seemed to be woven of vines and flowers. I crossed the silver-thread and mother-of-pearl bridge one moonlit midnight. I looked down into the melting heart of the world and saw my reflection in a bubble of fire while the harps sang and sighed and snarled around me with the very voice of the volcano.

Some day someone, perhaps my own child, may say that word of mine back to me — that word I said to my father — but I won't turn into a bridge. I shall become a journey winding over hills, across cities, along seashores and

through shrouded forests, crossing my father's bridges and
the bridges of other men, as well as all the infinitely divided
roads and splintered pathways that lie between them.

A Work of Art

Mrs Baskin's big son, Brian, was working in another city, but he was coming home for his birthday, so she decided to make him a rich fruitcake and to ice it herself. She had been taking cake-icing lessons at the Polytech for nearly a year and by now she felt she was rather good at it, better indeed than her instructor, who liked brightly coloured, frilly sort of icing. Mrs Baskin preferred something plainer and cooler. As she got out the cake mixing bowl, wooden spoon, a big plastic bowl for the dried fruit, the sifter for sifting the dry ingredients, as well as the big, hinged cake-tin, a picture came into her mind of how the cake might look: pure, almost — but not quite — unearthly, a cake that had been iced by moonlight on midsummer night. She looked at her calendar and saw with pleasure that it would be full moon that night.

Mrs Baskin set about things in a very orderly fashion. First she greased one side of the greaseproof paper with a knob of butter, and then she fitted it, butterside up, in the big, hinged cake-tin. She turned on the oven so that it would be heating while she worked. Then she put the dried fruit into the plastic bowl – currants, candied peel, sultanas, seedless raisins, a little bit of chopped ginger and almonds, as well as glacé cherries and crystallized angelica to give a bit of colour to the cake when it was sliced. Once she'd mixed the dried fruit, she floured it a little so the fruit wouldn't stick to itself. Then she sifted half a pound of plain flour and half a teaspoon of baking powder into yet another bowl, an old pottery one that had belonged to her mother.

Her three youngest children, Hamlet, Serena and Toby, watched her, for they were as interested in Brian's cake as if it were theirs, too. They were certain Brian would let them have some of it. Even Wellington, the dog, watched, wagging his tail whenever anyone spoke to him. Hubert, the cat, pretended to be asleep, but if you looked closely you could see two thin, green slits in his black face. He liked to know just what was going on in his house.

Mrs Baskin creamed butter and brown sugar until the mixture was light and fluffy, and then beat in four eggs, one at a time. She slowly added the flour, stirring as she went, and finally the fruit mixture. Her arm grew rather tired. Hamlet had a go, but he could scarcely move the spoon. Serena had a go, but she couldn't move it at all. Toby was too little even to try. He could barely stand, let alone stir a birthday cake. Not only that, he was teething and Mrs Baskin thought he might dribble into the mixture. Of course, Wellington and Hubert were no use at all.

Just then, the big girls, Audrey and Vanilla, came in from school, arguing and hitting each other with their school bags. But they stopped fighting when they saw that their mother was making a birthday cake. They quickly realized that there would be delicious cake mixture left on the inside of the mixing bowl.

"Mum, Mum, can I lick the bowl?" they cried together.

There was an immediate rush for the spoon drawer. Everyone but Toby grabbed a spoon. Mrs Baskin carefully scraped most of the mixture into her hinged cake-tin and put it in the oven.

At that moment one of the middle boys, Leonard, came in from cricket practice. Mrs Baskin gave him the mixing spoon to lick. Audrey said it wasn't fair. Vanilla said Serena was letting her hair drag in the bowl. Serena hit Hamlet with her spoon for taking too much. Hamlet pretended he was badly hurt, fell over backwards and knocked Toby over. Immediately, Wellington stood on everyone and began licking the bowl before anyone else.

After she had baked the cake for an hour and a half, Mrs Baskin lowered the oven temperature and baked it for a further two and a quarter hours. By the time it was ready to come out of the tin the other middle boy, Greville, came in. The bowl and the mixing spoon were washed and put away by then, but Greville didn't care. He had had a secret meal of fish and chips with his friend Simon, under Simon's bed. He liked the look of the cake though, and said he couldn't wait for Brian to get home.

When the cake was properly cool, Mrs Baskin brushed it with apricot glaze before covering it in almond paste. Then she drove Greville away from the television (the six youngest children were already in bed), made herself a cup of tea, turned the television off, and sat in the moony dark for a little while, getting herself into a magical, cake-icing mood. She had a short, refreshing sleep, then got up, washed her face and put on some make-up (so as to get in a birthday party mood). She thought about Brian who had been her first baby. She thought about him growing year by year, losing teeth, scraping his knees, learning how to ride a bike, going to college, and so on. The cake needed to be iced in such a way that anyone who saw it would somehow be aware of these things. She would not write *Happy Birthday* on it but she would ice it so that anyone who saw it would *feel* Happy Birthday-ish.

While she iced, the moon peered in at the window, looking rather like an iced cake itself. Mrs Baskin smiled and waved to it. She thought it looked surprised but pleased. When she had finished icing the cake she put it on a silver stand and then, because it seemed a pity to shut it away in a cake-tin, she covered it with a glass dome which had once belonged to her grandmother, and stood it on top of the piano. The moon looked in and touched it gently. The cake seemed to glow with a moony light of its own.

When the children saw the cake next morning they all stood and stared at it, astonished.

"Gee, Mum, it's too good to eat," said Greville, though he didn't really mean it.

The children who were old enough to go to school went to school; the little children played under the table. Mrs Baskin began to vacuum the house. The vacuum cleaner made a lot of noise and she did not hear the knock at the door, but Hamlet heard it. He opened the door and let two men in. One was dressed in a floppy, striped shirt and designer-jeans. The other wore an elegant suit.

"Excuse us," they said, "but we are the owners of the

art gallery down the road. We just happened to be passing and we saw that wonderful thing you have there on your piano. Is it yours?"

Mrs Baskin explained that it was hers in a way. She had made it. However, the real owner was her son, Brian, who would be coming home in a month's time.

"It's a very rich cake," she explained, "and it will improve over the next month. Cakes like these improve with keeping."

The gallery owners, who were both on permanent diets, did not know much about cakes. They were astonished to find the elegant sculpture they had admired through the window was actually an iced birthday cake.

"It has a certain look, a certain ambiance ... I don't know! What would you say, Wynstan?" asked the one in the striped, floppy, shirt, whose own name was Zachary.

"Purity!" said Wynstan. "What do you say, Zack? Shall we make an offer?"

They offered Mrs Baskin fifty dollars for her cake. She was certainly tempted. But it would not be full moon again for a month, and she had iced that cake at that special time in that special way for Brian. If she sold it she knew she could not make another one quite as good until it was full moon again.

"I'll rent it to you for fifty dollars," she said at last. "But you must get it insured against anyone eating it and you mustn't take it from under the glass dome or it'll get dusty."

She didn't think they would take up her offer but, after a lot of frowning and arguing, they did. There was something about that cake – they couldn't quite say what it was – but they were determined to display it in their gallery. They came round with a van later in the day and carried it off.

When the little ones saw the cake being carried off, they all began to cry. Mrs Baskin told them that it would be coming back again but they did not believe her. They were sure the gallery owners would take the cake into their gallery and then eat it all themselves. Being so small they didn't understand that it was insured.

The next morning, on the front page of the newspaper, there was a photograph of Mrs Baskin's cake. *Tour de force by Local Artist*, said a headline.

"It's not a *tour de force*," complained Audrey. "It's an iced cake."

"Gee, you're dumb," said Greville. "A *tour de force* means a – it means something terrific."

"You don't know what it means either!" said Vanilla, who always stuck up for Audrey when Audrey was arguing with Greville. Greville went into his room, pretending he didn't care, and looked up *tour de force* in the dictionary.

"*Tour de force* means feat of strength or skill, you noddy!" he said when he came back.

"Mum, Greville's calling me a noddy!" complained Audrey.

"That means I've got two *tour de forces*," said Leonard, dancing up and down. "Feet of skill and strength."

"Well, they smell pretty strong after you've been playing cricket," said Vanilla.

"That's enough of that," said Mrs Baskin. She had been trying to talk to someone on the phone. "Help me tidy the house! The television people are coming round."

The children were so impressed at the thought of being on television that they raced about helping their mother by turning cushions upside down so that the cat fur Hubert had left on them was underneath. But by half past eight the cameras had still not arrived and the big children had to go to school.

Mrs Baskin wished she had had time to get her hair set, but it was too late. She tore into the bathroom and put on some lipstick and eyeliner to brighten herself up a bit. The television people came in, Wellington barked himself hoarse, while Hubert panicked and shot up the curtains to hide on top of the bookshelf.

"When did you get the idea of using cake as an art form?" asked the television interviewer. "Is it a feminist protest against being a slave in the kitchen?"

"No, it's a birthday cake," said Mrs Baskin. "My son, Brian, is coming home for his birthday next month and I made a cake for him."

Mrs Baskin was on television that night. Apart from her hair, she thought she did pretty well, but she wasn't the only person on the programme. There was a man from the local university talking about her cake.

"What we see here is a return to folk art ... to the art of the *people*," he said. "It is functional art — this cake is meant to be *used*, and yet the artist shows instinctive awareness of texture and balance. She *interprets* the quality of *cakeness* and tests her creation against traditional concepts. Tradition is recognized, and yet I think we are witnessing the emergence of a new dynamic."

"Wow, Mum!" said Greville.

"Pretty cool!" said Vanilla. "But when are they going to bring that cake back?"

"Brian doesn't come home for a month," Mrs Baskin said. "That cake's probably safer there than it is here."

"You bet!" agreed Leonard, clashing his knife and fork, which encouraged all the little ones to clash their knives and forks, too.

"Now then," said Mrs Baskin, "that's enough of that! You kids can do the dishes. I'm going out."

"Where are you going?" asked Audrey.

"Just down the road to the gallery," said Mrs Baskin. "Greville will babysit. You can put Toby to bed, Leonard! Read Hamlet a story, Vanilla!"

She put on her best dress and went down to the gallery. Her iced cake looked very beautiful, very mysterious, sitting in the window. It looked a little like a lot of different things, but most of all it looked like something simple which somehow nobody had ever noticed until now. It was the mixture of looking like a lot of other things and looking like something entirely new that made it so astonishing. As well as all that it was a cake. Everyone liked it.

When Mrs Baskin stepped into the gallery, Zack and Wynstan ran to meet her. Zack kissed her right hand and Wynstan kissed her left, and Wynstan's mother came to tell her how thrilling her cake was.

"When I saw it, I said, that's *art!* I said, that's what art's about. It's a cake — yes — but not *just* a cake. It's a statement in its own right. My dear, it's got such passionate equilibrium."

Mrs Baskin talked to a lot of interesting people in the gallery, drank some sherry and ate a slice of another, inferior cake. She enjoyed herself and was able to check that her cake was being well looked after. The gallery was dust free and had controlled humidity.

The next day she had her hair set, and it was just as

well she did, for two reporters from art magazines came to talk to her, bringing photographers with them.

"I can't tell you how much I admire it," said one reporter. "The stand, the cake itself, and the dome, are all organized to make separate yet identical statements. You've somehow represented the finite universe, continuous in space, powerful in its defiance of causality, but threatened by entropy. And then there's the time dimension. Implicit in it are times we can define as *before cake* and *after cake*."

When they had gone, Mrs Baskin went down to the gallery again. She had to wait in a small queue that had formed in order to look at her cake. People stared through the glass longingly, and it took quite a while for the queue to move. At last it was Mrs Baskin's turn. As she filed past it she took a good, hard look at it. She saw that all the things the critics and reporters were saying could be quite true. She also saw that the cake was looking as fresh as ever and that there was no dust on it.

Over the next day or two Mrs Baskin received phone calls from London and New York. Certain art galleries were anxious to display her cake. Others were flying art critics over to write about it.

Vanilla and Audrey quickly learned to talk like art critics.

"Audrey, what do you think of the sculptural projection of this sandwich?" Vanilla would ask.

"I think it's visually significant," Audrey would say. "But the tomato's sliding out of it!"

"I made it like that on purpose," Vanilla cried, catching the tomato. "To give it immediacy."

"Gee, what a pair of noddys!" exclaimed Leonard.

"Noddys!" repeated Hamlet, pleased to join in talking to the big ones.

"Mum, Leonard's teaching Hamlet to call us noddys," shouted Audrey and Vanilla together.

Three weeks later it was announced that Mrs Baskin had won a medal for a significant contribution to new art. The President of the Society of Arts presented the medal and shook her hand.

"What a cake!" he cried. "It has a certain Byzantine quality, no?"

"Maybe ..." said Mrs Baskin. Once people had pointed out things about her cake to her she often saw them herself. Had they been there all the time? Or did people call them into being by naming them? And did it matter?

At the end of a fortnight there was a change of display at the gallery and her cake was sent home.

"But don't worry!" said Wynstan. "We have lots of openings for it. Let us be your agents: your cake has a brilliant career in front of it."

Never had his gallery been so full. Never had there been such queues or such enthusiasm. He and Zack were planning a great pikelet-and-jam exhibition. He could hear the critics now. "There is an effortless virtuosity about the way the jam is applied that takes the breath away," or, "The static alignment of the pikelet brings out the semi-fluid texture of the jam component."

He went home feeling very happy.

His mother had made him a pancake, not great art, but very tasty. Suddenly, the phone rang. Wynstan answered it. Within ten minutes he had leaped into his car and rushed around to get Zack. Within three minutes they were on their way to Mrs Baskin's.

They did not knock. They burst into her front room and found her among her children – Toby, Serena, Hamlet,

Audrey, Vanilla, Leonard and Greville. But there was one other. A tall, young man sat there with Hubert on his knees and Wellington under his chair. Everyone had a very well fed look.

Wynstan seized Mrs Baskin's hand.

"Wonderful news, dear!" he said. "I've just had a Japanese firm on the phone and they want to buy your cake for ten thousand."

"Ten thousand what?" asked Mrs Baskin.

"Dollars, pounds, yen . . . who cares!" cried Zack. "We'll only take fifteen per cent commission and the rest of that lovely lolly will be yours. Where is the cake?"

Mrs Baskin pointed.

What was left of it was in the middle of the table. The cherries and the angelica glowed like rubies and emeralds among the dark, rich crumbs.

"You've eaten it!" cried Wynstan. "You've eaten a work of art."

"We all did," said Brian (for the young man with Hubert on his knees was Brian). "It was my birthday cake!"

"But that wasn't just a cake. It was art!" cried Wynstan.

Mrs Baskin got up from the table.

"It was art," she agreed, "but it was also a cake – Brian's birthday cake. Some art is meant to last and some is meant to be eaten up. Not everything has to be a monument."

"It was terrific cake," said Brian. "Have some?"

Wynstan and Zack looked hungrily at the cake.

"Well, maybe just a crumb," said Zack, accepting a large slice. Later, both he and Wynstan had to admit it was the best-tasting art they had ever come across.

Mrs Baskin watched everyone enjoying the cake and thought of her big, hinged cake-tin, the plastic bowl, the pottery bowl, and the big mixing bowl waiting quietly in the dark cupboard, and a mysterious excitement stirred in her.

"I'll make another cake tomorrow ... but not a birthday cake. You can't make the same cake twice," she thought to herself, and she glanced at the calendar. Four weeks had gone by surprisingly quickly. Tomorrow night the moon would be full again.

The Wind Between the Stars

One day, when Phoebe was small, her old Granny came in shaking her head and saying, "The wind's blowing from right between the stars tonight." Little Phoebe stopped playing and listened to the wind. It sounded big enough to snatch up the hills in its right hand and the moon in its left, and to carry them away for always.

"From right between the stars?" Phoebe asked.

"Three times around the world and off again," said her Granny. "Off between the stars — and if anyone wants to go with it, it will take them — yes — but they mustn't hope to come back again. That's the way of the wind from between the stars."

Phoebe lay in her bed and listened to that wind. She thought she heard pattering feet and laughter, and tears and singing and fingers scratching at the window.

'Shall I open my window,' thought little Phoebe, 'in case

the wind doesn't ever blow from between the stars again?'

Her bed was warm and she was sleepy. Betwixt the beginning and the end of her thought she fell asleep, and the wind from between the stars blew around the world three times and went off again without her.

Phoebe grew up to be a young girl with wild, black hair and long, dancing legs. She ran like a hare over the springtime hills, racing the wind that blew in from the sea. She laughed to feel the new grass under her bare feet, and to smell the scents of the sea and earth the wind carried with it. At her side ran Michael, her friend, strong and brown as a tree, nimble as a goat.

"I've never been so happy," said Phoebe, laughing and looking at the world through the net of her own tangled hair. "We've raced the wind, Michael. We've left it behind."

"I can hear it coming after us," Michael said. "Listen!"

Far away, Phoebe heard the wind murmuring and saw the trees bend before it. Suddenly it changed. Its note grew deeper and stronger. It boomed like a solemn drum, and yet it piped a high music, shrill and clear.

"It's singing!" Phoebe called. "It's singing." She heard the laughter and the tears and the pattering feet. But Michael took her hand and started to run down the hill, pulling her after him.

"Why," said Phoebe, "it's that wind back again — the wind from between the stars. Stop, Michael. Stop and listen, Michael."

Michael would not stop. "It's not a usual sort of wind," he cried. "It may mean trouble. It's best to be inside when it comes."

Phoebe ran with him, half willing, half sorry. Before the

door of her grandmother's cottage shut her safely in, she peeped back over her shoulder and saw, in a somersault second, the wind whirling a few leaves down the street behind her. It sang its huge song, and Phoebe thought she saw – just perhaps – a whole crowd of people streaming and dancing down the street, people so strange she thought she must have dreamed them in the dark blink of an eye.

The wind blew and sang three times around the world and then was off, out between the stars again.

Phoebe stayed behind. She married Michael and they had six children and a happy life together. Slowly her wild, black hair was tamed – at last it was all held down with net and pins – it began to turn white. Slowly her long legs forgot how to dance, and Phoebe hid them under petticoats, a skirt and an apron. Her children grew up and went away and one day Michael died, an old man. Phoebe was all alone. She did not have much money, so she went to work for Miss Gibb who lived in a tall, white house a mile out of the village.

Miss Gibb matched her house. She was tall and cold and white. No wild flowers or unruly grass grew around Miss Gibb's house, and there were no wild flowers or untidy corners in her heart either. She lived alone with the hundred beautiful dresses she had worn when she was young. She did not wear them now, but she thought of them, and took them down and looked at them, or stroked them as they hung in their long rows.

"Do you remember?" she whispered – and the silk whispered back, *Remember, remember.*

Phoebe had never met anyone as cold and white and tall as Miss Gibb. Doing just whatever Miss Gibb told her to do, she scuttled around like a frightened little mouse, not daring to talk or smile, or even to look at Miss Gibb. Miss Gibb always looked over Phoebe's head as if she were staring into some ruined garden, or a world where it is always winter.

One day, Miss Gibb smelled honeysuckle and mignonette in the air. She decided her dresses would like to be out in the sun and told Phoebe to take them down from their wardrobe and hang them on the line. There was not room on the line for them all. Phoebe hung most of them under the trees where they swayed like big flowers – like great bunches of bright fruit. Miss Gibb's neat garden blossomed out in a strange summer of silk and velvet, lace, chiffon, muslin, taffeta and satin. The whole garden murmured and sighed, waking to rustling life as the breeze moved among the dresses.

Phoebe went into Miss Gibb's room to bring out the last dresses. She put them over her arm and was about to carry them out into the garden when suddenly she saw her reflection in the mirror opposite. Phoebe hadn't seen herself in such a fine mirror for a long time, and she stopped, amazed. Who was that little withered creature shuffling along, white-haired and faded? What had happened to Phoebe, the little girl dancing in front of the winter fire, or to long-legged Phoebe running over the hills, watching the world through a net of black hair? A net of wrinkles sat over Phoebe's face now and she had forgotten how to dance.

'Yet,' thought Phoebe, 'I don't feel so different. I'm still the same. Here I am. Here I am. But who is there to remember me? Who is there left to call me by my name, Phoebe, to know who I really am, and to see the real me looking out from behind all these wrinkles?' Then an idea came to her. 'I wonder if I can still dance?'

Phoebe tucked up her petticoats a bit and began to dance. Stiff and old as they were, Phoebe's feet remembered their dancing. They fell happily into the old, gay steps and Phoebe danced, still light on her toes, like a tune on a squeaky penny whistle, or a little spiral of dust lifting in the summer wind.

"See," said Phoebe to the old Phoebe in the glass. "I'm still there!" She turned on her toes and nearly banged into Miss Gibb standing stone-still, icicle-cold, in the doorway.

"Really, Mrs Moffat," said Miss Gibb, using Phoebe's other name and speaking in a small, chilly voice. "Do you have to do your prancing here all over my carpet in front of my mirror?"

Poor Phoebe felt lost.

'Nobody knows me,' she thought. 'They only know that little old woman in the mirror – and this isn't so surprising, because that's who I really am.'

"I'm sorry, miss," she said to Miss Gibb. "I don't know what came over me."

"Make sure it doesn't come over you again," Miss Gibb said. "And for goodness sake, be careful of my dresses."

Phoebe looked at Miss Gibb and suddenly saw that Miss Gibb, too, spent long times in front of her mirror staring, bewildered, wondering what had happened to the girl who had worn those hundred beautiful dresses, who had once been loved and admired.

"This getting old, miss," said Phoebe, "it's a terrible hard thing, but it comes to everyone."

Miss Gibb looked over Phoebe's head, out of the window into the sunny garden, but her eyes reflected a winter that wasn't really there. "Do the work you are paid

to do, Mrs Moffat, and don't chatter." Out in the garden
the dresses suddenly moved on the trees and a deeper
murmur was heard stirring and growing.

"The wind!" Miss Gibb said. "How annoying! Bring my
dresses in at once, Mrs Moffat." But Phoebe stood quite
still and listened.

"The wind!" she said. "The wind from between the
stars."

It came over the house like a great wave and the dresses
under the trees broke free, and soared and swirled around,
high up around the chimney, curtsying and bowing,
mopping and mowing, in the air. They seemed worn by
unseen, laughing people.

"Shut the window!" screamed Miss Gibb. "The wind
will take us all!"

"Open the window," said Phoebe. "The wind can take
me if it wants to, along with all its other dead leaves."

"Mrs Moffat, close the window!" said Miss Gibb. But
Phoebe was beyond all fearing. All she could feel was
happiness – someone knew her, someone had remembered
her, someone knew what she really was, and had called to
remind her.

"Miss Gibb! Don't be scared, Miss Gibb," Phoebe cried.
She flung the window open and the wind filled the whole
house.

It rang with sounds of laughter and song and carried
with it the company of people it had collected around the
world and in and out of the stars. Kings crowned with ears
of corn and crimson poppies, peacocks, mermaids, comets,
the twelve dancing princesses, dragonflies, Helen of Troy,
lyre birds, minstrels with lutes, gypsies to tell your fortune,
little silver fish, frogs and roses, Rapunzel – wound around

in her own shining hair – the crippled lizard-beggarman from near Alpha Centauri. There were laughing lions, their manes plaited with flowers, centaurs, and vast shadowy people with wings. Some faces smiled and some wept, as all these people wandered and wavered, melted and moved on the huge breath of the wind. Dancing among them went Miss Gibb's hundred dresses, but whether they were worn by unseen wind people or just tossed by the wind, who can say?

"Oh!" cried Phoebe. "Here I am. Here I am!"

"Well, we've waited long enough for you," said a lion. "Twice we've come looking for you, but you always wanted to do something else. Now take your feet off the ground and come too."

Phoebe laughed breathlessly. "May I? Can I?"

"Try," said a king who, sighing past her, smelt of autumn and of sun shining on ripe corn. Phoebe stepped, danced, and then, in her dance, lifted her feet off the ground. Slowly the wind took her, turned her over upside-down, around, around . . .

Phoebe squeaked like a little mouse, "Oh! Oh! I'm upside-down!"

"It's a wonderful way to see the world," said a princess, hanging head down beside her, tapping her worn dancing shoes on the ceiling before she slowly turned head over heels softly down. Her place was taken by a row of Miss Gibb's dancing dresses – the pink, foaming, bubbling organza, the sleek, black velvet, the tender, shimmering silk looking like silver tears. They bowed to Phoebe, but she could only wave back, for it was her turn to slide down the lap of the wind to bob and laugh with the shy mermaids, to hold in her hands for a moment the scaly paw of the

56

lizard-beggar, to vanish in a swirling spiral of leaves and rose petals.

"Going ..." said the wind. "We're going ... we can't wait!"

"But, Miss Gibb!" Phoebe called. "Let Miss Gibb come too."

"Take your feet off the ground, Miss Gibb," called the lions and the mermaids. But no, Miss Gibb could not take her feet from the ground. She could only stare and snatch at her dancing dresses.

And the wind, the wind from between the stars, took them as it takes all things that flow and are free. Carrying Phoebe on its back, riding her along like a queen in triumph, it swept three times around the world and off, out, between the stars once more... If anyone wants to go with it, it will take them, but they mustn't hope to come back again.

Perdita and Maddy

One day, Perdita Hoddinott came home from changing her library books and found a letter in the box. It was not often that anything as interesting as that happened to Perdita. She looked at the rollicking writing which covered the entire envelope, leaving scarcely any room for the stamp, and saw at once that it was from her adventurous sister, Maddy, whom she had not seen for years. Perdita made herself a cup of tea, put on her glasses, and settled down to read the letter.

"Dear Perdita," the letter read. "I have sprained my ankle during a nasty incident with an enraged water-buffalo. I am therefore giving up my life of adventure and coming home to spend my last days in the sunshine of Pemberton Falls. I am longing to see you. Put a hot-water bottle in my bed and lay in some lemons, please. I have a slight cold because of falling into Arctic waters. Never again will I try to help a walrus in difficulty.

They are stupid, ungrateful animals. Your loving sister, Maddy."

"Oh, dear," sighed Perdita. "What on earth will Maddy find to do here? Pemberton Falls is such a quiet place."

This was true. Pemberton Falls was a small, quiet town, though the town council was always trying to attract tourists by sticking up posters with pictures of the town waterfall on it. It was a good waterfall as waterfalls go, but there was nothing much in Pemberton Falls *except* the waterfall and the bridge crossing it: no maddened water-buffalo and no walruses — stupid or otherwise. It was hard to imagine Maddy settling down happily in Pemberton Falls.

Maddy arrived the following day by parachute, cleverly holding her sprained ankle up in the air. She landed on her enormous crutches which had special springs on them to cushion the shock. As soon as she had stopped bouncing up and down she gave Perdita a big hug. Her sprained ankle was all strapped up, and she carried a box of paper handkerchiefs. Maddy was glad to sink into a pretty bed which had a hot-water bottle in it and a nice view of the waterfall from the bedroom window. Perdita sat beside her, knitting, while, in between sneezes, Maddy described her adventures with volcanoes, and told her about visiting the dangerous island of Kakkamungo, and meeting the great white shark in the waters off Fiji.

"If I hadn't had my umbrella with me, I wouldn't be here to tell the tale," Maddy cried dramatically, her hair standing on end with the excitement of her own story. "And, as you know, it's almost unheard of for a skin diver to have an umbrella when diving. I looked at the water and thought ... shall I, or shall I not? And then I decided ..."

"Maddy, dear," said Perdita. "You must tell me all about it when I come home. I have to go down to the library now to change some books, and I thought I might buy a nice fillet of fish on the way home."

"What am I to do while you're away?" cried Maddy. "It won't be very interesting for me lying here in bed, with nothing to look at but the waterfall!"

Perdita could see that Maddy needed entertainment, but how could she entertain an adventurous sister when she had to go down to the library to change some books? Then she had a sudden idea.

"I will teach you to knit," she said, "and you can begin knitting squares for a patchwork bed-cover while I'm away."

Fortunately, Maddy liked the bright colours. It took her quite a long time to get used to the needles, for she held them as if they were underwater spear-guns. But at last Perdita said, "Now, just continue like that, Maddy. You'll soon get the hang of it, and when I come home I will show you how to cast off."

"Hurry back," said Maddy, concentrating hard on her knitting.

Perdita changed her books at the Pemberton Falls library and had a bit of a gossip with the librarian. Then she stopped at the fish shop and bought two nice fillets of fish, as well as scraps for her cats, and set off home. She had done this many, many times and nothing remarkable had ever happened. But there is always a first time for everything, of course.

As she went over the bridge she was suddenly attacked by a hungry fish-hawk. Striking at the bird with her shopping bag, she lost her balance and fell heavily against the railings of the bridge. Under its smart paint the railing was quite rotten. It cracked and gave way. Perdita went head over heels, right over the falls.

She plunged deep into the pool at the bottom of the falls which was full of junk untidy picnickers had thrown into the stream, and desperately seized an old picnic basket with a broken handle that was bobbing around there. She held on so tightly that even when she fainted, her grip was still strong. Holding fast to the picnic basket, Perdita was washed down the stream into a swift river and then far out to sea.

There she was rescued by the crew of a yacht who were on a round-the-world yacht race. They were in the lead, but not by very much, and of course they did not want to waste time taking her back to land. So on they sailed, taking Perdita with them.

Meanwhile, Maddy was waiting impatiently for Perdita to come home so she could describe more of her adventures. After all, there's not much use in having adventures if there's nobody to listen to them. If she had been looking at the beautiful view of the falls she might have seen Perdita tumble over, but she was concentrating on her knitting, determined to get the hang of it.

Once on board, Perdita quickly recovered, of course. But a very strange thing had happened. What with the fall, and the shock of the cold water, Perdita had quite forgotten who she was. All she could remember were the stories Maddy had been telling her just before that fatal expedition to change the library books. Those stories now seemed like memories to poor, confused Perdita.

"The last thing I can remember is fighting the great white shark," she said frowning. "It's lucky I had my

umbrella with me, for as you know it's very rare for skin-divers to take an umbrella with them ..."

As they listened to her stories, the round-the-world yachtsmen became very excited. "What a wonderful addition she would make to our crew," they muttered to one another. "We badly need a shark expert."

"But I know nothing of yachts," said Perdita. "Nothing that I can remember."

"You'll soon get the hang of it," said the captain of the round-the-world crew. "We'll teach you to take in the spinnaker and cast off."

"Teach me to cast off," murmured Perdita. "I think I know how to cast off already." The words sounded familiar and, as far as she knew, she had nothing better to do, so she joined the crew and set off around the world without further to-do.

Meanwhile, Maddy had been forced to get up and cook something for herself. Grumbling and limping, she made a rather tough, flat chocolate cake, then got back into bed and ate it while she knitted. By now she was knitting with greater ease. Her knitting was already quite long but, of course, she couldn't cast off so she had no choice but to keep going.

There isn't room to tell you of all the adventures Perdita had over the next ten years, but you can borrow books from the library and read about them. She and the other members of the yacht crew won the round-the-world race. They were presented with a big cup, and were featured in several television advertisements. Perdita bought herself a Piper Cherokee aeroplane with her share of the prize money, got her pilot's licence, and set off round the world again, taking the picnic basket full of nutritious sandwiches with her. She not only fought with pirates in the China Sea, but did a lot of exploring as well. For instance, she was the first person to fly a Piper Cherokee aircraft down into the crater of the volcano on the island of Kakkamungo. She also took part in the library riots in the great city of Hookywalker, and she made friends with many gorillas, pythons and tigers in all parts of the world. When skin-diving off Fiji she took her umbrella, and nobody ever knew why. Nobody recognized, for that matter, either Perdita or the picnic basket when they appeared on television, because she had lost a lot of weight and the picnic basket's handle had been mended.

Then, one day when she was walking through the market place – in Kakkamungo, funnily enough – she saw an old woman sitting on a barrel, knitting.

Before she knew what she was doing she thought, I must get home and show Maddy how to cast off.

Maddy? Cast off? In a rush her memory came back to her. She had left poor Maddy with a sprained ankle and no dinner, and had not even shown her how to cast off. Perdita ran for her Piper Cherokee aircraft at once, fuelled, did a rapid engine check, and set off for Pemberton Falls immediately. She landed at the nearest airport and was just going to telephone for a taxi when a bright poster caught her eye. PEMBERTON FALLS, the poster said. SEE THE LONGEST PIECE OF KNITTING IN THE WORLD. SEE ALSO THE BEAUTIFUL WATERFALL, AND VISIT THE CHOCOLATE CAKE TEA-ROOM. BUS LEAVES IN TEN MINUTES.

Could it be the same Pemberton Falls? she wondered. Or were there two of them? A lot can happen in ten years. Perdita climbed on to the bus with several other tourists.

Sure enough it was the same Pemberton Falls that she remembered, but much, much busier. There were tourists everywhere, walking up and down the main street, looking at a long strip of knitting in all colours. It stretched down the main road winding several times round each lamp post, across the falls and past the library ... there seemed no end to it. It went on and on and on and on like a thin, stretched-out rainbow. At last it turned in at a gateway, up a drive and in at a back door. Perdita recognized the back door, for it was her very own back door. She followed the knitting in and discovered the whole bottom floor of the house was now a beautiful tea-room, full of tourists drinking tea and gorging themselves on large slices of chocolate cake.

TWO DOLLARS TO SEE THE FAMOUS KNITTING WOMAN OF PEMBERTON FALLS, proclaimed a notice. Perdita had to pay to go up her own stairs and there, in bed, with her foot still bandaged up, was Maddy — knitting furiously. Even while Perdita stood in the doorway she knitted another two inches. She had certainly got the hang of it!

"Oh, Perdita," Maddy cried. "I'm *so* pleased to see you. I've missed you so much. When your library books were found in the pool at the bottom of the falls, I feared the worst. I knitted and knitted to keep myself from brooding. It's such a demanding life what with all this knitting to do, and baking the chocolate cakes at night. But don't you worry about a thing. I've paid for the library books, and I've kept the wolf from the door. I'd rather work with wolves than walruses any day. Ring for tea and chocolate cake and I'll tell you all my adventures."

"How is your poor ankle? Still sprained?" cried Perdita.

"Oh, no!" cried Maddy, frowning at her bandage. "I had an unpleasant encounter with a dog, a most ungrateful and ill-tempered hound. I had taken half an hour off from my knitting, and was quietly walking over the bridge to change the library books, when two dogs began to fight right in front of me. Well, I wasn't going to put up with that so I seized my umbrella and ..."

One of the girls from the tea-room brought in a cup of tea and a slice of delicious chocolate cake. Perdita sat down in the chair by Maddy's bed.

How funny, she thought. *I* learned to cast off and Maddy didn't. How different sisters can be!

And, as she sat there, listening peacefully to all Maddy's knitting-adventures and looking out of the window at the beautiful view of Pemberton Falls, Perdita suddenly felt delighted that life was full of surprises. How good it was never to know what was going to happen next!

The House of Coloured Windows

Our street had a lot of little houses on either side of it where we children lived happily with our families. There were rows of lawns, like green napkins tucked under the houses' chins, and letterboxes, apple trees and marigolds. Children played up and down the street, laughing and shouting and sometimes crying, for it's the way of the world that things should be mixed. In the soft autumn evenings, before the winter winds began, the smoke from chimneys rose up in threads of grey and blue, stitching our houses into the autumn air.

But there was one house in our street that was different from all the rest, and that was the wizard's house. For one thing there was a door knocker of iron in the shape of a dog's head that barked at us as we ran by. Of course, the wizard's house had its lawn too, but no apple trees or marigolds, only a silver tree with a golden parrot in it. But that was not the most wonderful thing about the wizard's house.

Once, we saw a tiny dragon sitting on the wizard's compost heap among the apple cores, weeds and egg shells. He scratched under a green wing with a scarlet claw and breathed out blue flames and grey smoke. We saw the wizard shaking his tablecloth out of the window. Bits of old spells and scraps of magic flew into the air like pink confetti, blue spaghetti and bits and bobs of rainbow. As they fell, they went off like fireworks and only coloured dust reached the ground. The hot sun dissolved the dust as hot tea dissolves sugar. But still those things were not the real wonders of the wizard's house.

The real wonders of the wizard's house were its windows. They were all the colours of the world — red, blue, green, gold, purple and pink, violet and yellow, as well as the reddish-brown of autumn leaves. His house was patched all over with coloured windows. And there was not just one pink window or one green one, either, but several of each colour, each one different. No one had told us but we all knew that if you looked through the red window you saw a red world. If you looked through the blue window a blue one. The wizard could go into any of these worlds whenever he wished. He was not only the owner of many windows, but the master of many worlds.

My friend, Anthea, longed to go into the wizard's house and spy out through his windows. Other people dreamed of racing-bikes and cameras and guitars, but Anthea dreamed of the wizard's windows. She wanted to get into the wizard's house and look through first one window and then another because she was sure that through one of them she must see the world she really wanted to live in.

The candyfloss window would show her a world striped like circus time, the golden window would show her a city of towers and domes, dazzling in the sunlight, and every girl who lived there would be a princess with long golden hair. The windows haunted Anthea so much that her eyes ached for magic peep-holes into strange and beautiful countries.

One day, as Anthea came home from school, she saw on the footpath outside the wizard's house, sitting by his letterbox, a white cat with one blue eye and one green eye, golden whiskers and a collar of gold. It winked at her with its blue eye and scrambled through a gap in the hedge, seeming to beckon with its tail. Anthea scrambled after it with a twist and a wriggle and, when she stood up, she was on the other side of the hedge inside the wizard's garden. Her school uniform had been changed into a long, silver dress with little glass bells all over its sleeves, and her school shoes and socks had changed into slippers of scarlet and stockings of green. In front of her stood the wizard, dressed in a white robe with a tiny green dragon crawling around his shoulders. His cat rubbed against his ankles and purred.

"So, you are the girl who dreams of looking through my windows," said the wizard. "Your wishes are like storms, my dear — too strong, too strong. At night I am beginning to dream your dreams instead of my own and that won't do, for wizards need their own dreams to prevent them becoming lost in their magic. Dreams are to wizards what harbour lights are to a sailor. I'll let you look through my windows, and choose the world you like best of all, so long as you remember that when you walk out of my door you'll walk out into the world you have chosen,

and there'll be no coming back a second time. Be sure you choose well."

Anthea followed the wizard up the path between borders of prize-winning geraniums and in at his door.

"This is a lovely dress," she said to the wizard. "I feel halfway to being a princess already. It's much, much nicer than my school uniform."

"But it *is* a school uniform — the uniform of *my* school," the wizard replied in surprise. "I'm glad you like it. Now, here is the red window. Look well, my dear."

Anthea looked through the red window. She was looking deep into a forest on the sun. Trees blazed up from a wide plain and over a seething hillside. Their leaves were flames, and scarlet smoke rose up from the forest, filling the sky. Out from under the trees galloped a herd of fiery horses, tossing burning manes and tails and striking sparks from the ground with their smouldering hooves.

"Well?" asked the wizard.

"It's beautiful," breathed Anthea, "but it's much too hot."

The next window was a silver one. A princess, with a young face and long white hair, rode through a valley of snow in a silver sleigh drawn by six great white bears wearing collars of frost and diamonds. All around her, mountains rose like needles of silver ice into a blue, clear sky.

"Your silver window is beautiful," Anthea sighed, "but, oh — how cold, how cold! I couldn't live there."

Through a candyfloss-pink window, sure enough, she looked into a world of circuses. A pink circus tent opened like a spring tree in blossom. Clowns turned cartwheels around it, and a girl in a pink dress and pink slippers rode

73

on a dappled horse, jumping through a hoop hung with pink ribbons.

"That's funny!" Anthea said in a puzzled voice. "It's happy and funny and very, very pretty, but I wouldn't want to live with a circus every day. I don't know why not, but I just wouldn't."

That's how it was with all the windows. The blue one looked under the sea, and the green one into a world of treetops. There was a world of deserts and a world of diamonds, a world of caves and glow-worms, and a world of sky with floating cloud-castles, but Anthea did not want to live in any of them. She began to run from one window to another, the glass bells on her sleeves jingling and tinkling, her feet in the scarlet slippers sliding under her.

"Where is a window for me?" cried Anthea. She peered through windows into lavender worlds full of mist, worlds where grass grew up to the sky and spiders spun bridges with rainbow-coloured silk, into worlds where nothing grew and where great stones lay like a city of abandoned castles reaching from one horizon to another.

At last there were no windows left. The wizard's house had many, many windows, but Anthea had looked through them all and there was no world in which she wanted to live. She didn't want a hot one or a cold one, a wet one or a dry one. She didn't want a world of trees or a world of stones. The wizard shrugged his shoulders.

"You're hard to please," he said.

"But I wanted the very best one. I know I'd know the best one if only you'd let me see it. Isn't there one window left? One little window?"

"Funnily enough there is one window, but I didn't think you'd be interested," the wizard said. "You see ..."

"Please show it to me," begged Anthea.

"I ought to explain . . ." began the wizard.

"Please!" cried Anthea.

The wizard pointed at a little blue-and-white checked curtain. "Behind there," he said.

Anthea ran to pull it aside and found herself looking through a window as clear as a drop of rain water. She saw a little street with little houses on either side of it. Smoke went up, up, up, stitching the street into the autumn sky, and up and down the footpath children ran, shouting and laughing, though some were also crying. There was a woman very like Anthea's own mother, looking for someone very like Anthea, because dinner was ready and there were sausages and mashed potatoes waiting to be eaten.

"That's the one!" cried Anthea, delighted. "Why did you keep it until last? I've wasted a lot of time on other windows when this one was the best all the time."

Without waiting another moment, she ran out of the wizard's door, squeezed through the hedge and found herself in the street wearing her own school uniform again.

"Well, that's funny!" said the wizard to his cat. "Did you see that? She went back to the world she came out of in the first place. That's her mother taking her home for dinner. I must say they do look very happy."

Ten minutes later the white cat with the gold collar brought him a tray with his dinner on it. The wizard looked pleased.

"Oh boy!" he said, because he was having sausages and mashed potatoes, too.

And that night the wizard dreamed his own dreams once more, while Anthea dreamed of a racing-bike. And in the darkness, the wizard's house of many windows twinkled like a good spell amid the street lights that marched like bright soldiers down our street.

The Hookywalker
Dancers

In the heart of the great city of Hookywalker was the School of Dramatic Art. It was full of all sorts of actors and singers and wonderful clowns, but the most famous of them all was the great dancer, Brighton.

Brighton could leap like an antelope and spin like a top. He was as slender as a needle. In fact, when he danced you almost expected little stitches to follow him across the stage. Every day he did his exercises at the barre to music played on his tape-recorder.

"One and a plié and a stretch, two-three, and port de bras and back to first!" he counted. He exercised so gracefully that, outside the School of Dramatic Art, pedlars rented ladders so that lovers of the dance could climb up and look through the window at Brighton practising.

Of course, life being what it is, many other dancers were often jealous of him. I'm afraid that most of them ate too

much and were rather fat, whereas Brighton had an elegant figure. They pulled his chair away from under him when he sat down, or tried to trip him up in the middle of his dancing, but Brighton was so graceful he simply made falling down look like an exciting new part of the dance, and the people standing on ladders clapped and cheered and banged happily on the windows.

Although he was such a graceful dancer, Brighton was not conceited. He led a simple life. For instance, he didn't own a car, travelling everywhere on roller skates, his tape-recorder clasped to his ear. Not only this, he did voluntary work for the Society for Bringing Happiness to Dumb Beasts. At the weekends he would put on special performances for pets and farm animals. Savage dogs became quiet as lambs after watching Brighton dance, and nervous sheep grew wool thicker than ever before. Farmers from outlying districts would ring up the School of Dramatic Art and ask if they could hire Brighton to dance to their cows, and many a parrot, temporarily off its seed, was brought back to full appetite by seeing Brighton dance the famous solo called *The Noble Savage in the Lonely Wood*.

Brighton had a way of kicking his legs up that suggested deep sorrow, and his demi-pliés regularly brought tears to the eyes of the parrots, after which they tucked into their seed quite ravenously.

One day, the director of the School for Dramatic Art called Brighton to his office.

"Brighton," he said, "I have an urgent request here from a farmer who needs help with a flock of very nervous sheep. He is in despair!"

"Glad to help!" said Brighton in his graceful fashion. "What seems to be the trouble?"

"Wolves — that's what the trouble is!" cried the director. "He lives on the other side of the big forest, and a pack of twenty wolves comes out of the forest early every evening and tries to devour some of his prize merinos. It's disturbing the sheep very badly. They get nervous twitches, and their wool is falling out from shock."

"I'll set off at once," Brighton offered. "I can see it's an urgent case."

"It's a long way," the director said, doubtfully. "It's right on the other side of the forest."

"That's all right," said Brighton. "I have my trusty roller skates, and the road is tarred all the way. I'll take my tape-recorder to keep me company, and I'll get there in next to no time."

"That's very fast," the director said in a respectful voice. "Oh, Brighton, I wish all my dancers were like you! Times are hard for the School of Dramatic Art. A lot of people are staying at home and watching car crashes on television. They don't want art — they want danger, they want battle, murder and sudden death — and it's becoming much harder to run the school at a profit. If all our dancers were as graceful as you there would be no problem at all, but as you know a lot of them are just a whisker on the fat side. They don't do their exercises the way they should."

Little did he realize that the other dancers were actually listening at the key hole, and when they heard this critical remark they all began to sizzle with jealousy. You could hear them sizzling with it. "I'll show him who's fat and who isn't," muttered a very spiteful dancer called Antoine. "Where are Brighton's skates?"

Brighton's skates were, in fact, in the cloakroom under the peg on which he hung his beret and his great billowing cape. It was but the work of a moment to loosen one or two vital grommets. The skates looked all right, but they were no longer as safe as skates ought to be.

"There," said Antoine, laughing nastily. "They'll hold together for a little bit, but once he gets into the forest they'll collapse, and we'll see how he gets on then, all alone with the wind and the wolves — and without wheels."

The halls of the School of Dramatic Art rang with the jealous laughter of the other dancers as they slunk off in all directions. A minute later Brighton came in, suspecting nothing, put on his beret and his great billowing cape, strapped on his skates, and set off holding his tape-recorder to his ear.

Now, during the day the wolves spent a long time snoozing and licking their paws clean in a clearing on top of the hill. From there they had a good view of the Hookywalker road. They could look out in all directions and even see as far as Hookywalker when the air was clear. It happened that their present king was a great thinker, and something was worrying him deeply.

"I know we're unpopular," sighed the King of the Wolves, "but what can I do about it? It's in the nature of things that wolves steal a few sheep here and there. It's part of the great pattern of nature." Though this seemed reasonable he was frowning and brooding as he spoke. "Sometimes — I don't know — I feel there must be more to life than just ravening around grabbing the odd sheep and howling at the moon."

"Look!" cried the wolf who was on look-out duty. "Someone is coming down the great road from the city."

"How fast he's going!" said another wolf. "And whatever is it he is holding to his ear?"

"Perhaps he has earache," suggested a female wolf in compassionate tones. None of the wolves had ever seen a tape-recorder before.

"Now then, no feeling sorry for him," said the King of the Wolves. "You all know the drill. We get down to the edge of the road, and at the first chance we tear him to pieces. That's all part of the great pattern of nature I was mentioning a moment ago."

"That'll take his mind off his earache," said one of the wolves with a fierce, sarcastic snarl.

As the sun set majestically in the west, Brighton, his cloak billowing round him like a private storm cloud, reached the great forest. It was like entering another world, for a mysterious twilight reigned under the wide branches, a twilight without moon or stars. Tall, sombre pines looked down as if they feared the worst. But Brighton skated on, humming to himself. He was listening to the music of *The Noble Savage* and was waiting for one of the parts he liked best. Indeed, so busy was he humming and counting the beats that he did not notice a sudden wobble in his wheels. However, a moment after the wobble, his skates gave a terrible screech and he was pitched into the pine needles by the side of the road.

"Horrakapotchkin!" cried Brighton. "My poor skates!" (It was typical of this dancer that his first thought was for others.) However, his second thought was of the forest and the wolves that might be lurking there. It occurred to him that they might be tired of merino sheep, and would fancy a change of diet.

"Quick thought! Quick feet!" he said, quoting an old dancing proverb. He rushed around collecting a pile of firewood and pine cones, and then lit a good-sized fire there on the roadside. It was just as well he did, because when he looked up he saw the forest was alight with fiery red eyes. The wolves had arrived. They stole out of the forest and sat down on the edge of the fire light, staring at him very hard, all licking their lips in a meaningful way.

Brighton did not panic. Quietly, he rewound his tape-recorder to the very beginning, and then stood up coolly and began to do his exercises. A lesser dancer might have started off dancing straight away, but Brighton knew the greatest challenge of his life was ahead of him. He preferred to take things slowly and warm up properly in case he needed to do a few tricky steps before the night was out.

The wolves looked at each other uneasily. The king hesitated. There was something so tuneful about the music and so graceful about Brighton's dancing that he would have liked to watch it for a bit longer, but he knew he was part of nature's great plan, and must help his pack to tear Brighton to pieces. So he gave the order. "Charge!"

As one wolf the wolves ran towards Brighton, snarling and growling, but to their astonishment Brighton did not run away. No! He actually ran towards them and then, leaped up in the air — up, up and right over them — his cloak streaming out behind him. It had the words *Hookywalker School of Dramatic Art* painted on it. The wolves were going so fast that they could not stop themselves until they were well down the road. Brighton, meanwhile, landed with a heroic gesture, wheeled around, and then went on with his exercises, watching the wolves narrowly.

Once again, the wolves charged, and once again Brighton leaped. This time he jumped even higher, and the

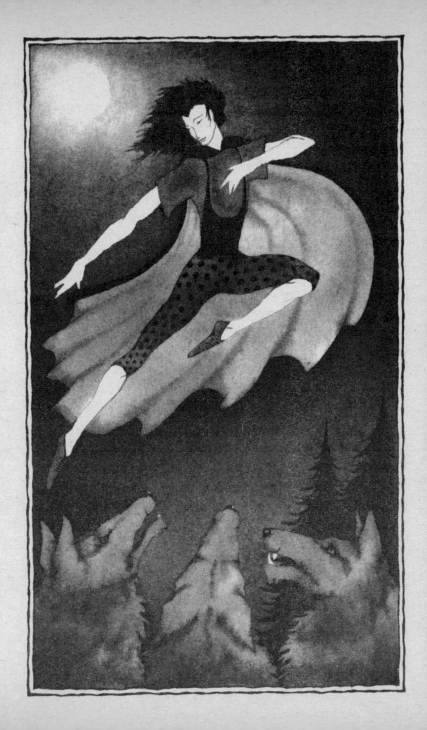

wolves couldn't help gasping in admiration, much as they hated missing out on any prey.

"Right!" cried the King of the Wolves. "Let's run round him in ever-decreasing circles." (This was an old wolf trick.) "He'll soon be too giddy to jump." However, being a wolf and not used to classical ballet, the king didn't realize that a good dancer can spin on his toes without getting in the least bit giddy. Brighton spun until he was a mere blur and actually rose several inches in the air with the power of his rotation. It was the wolves who became giddy first; they stumbled over one another, ending up in a heap, with their red eyes all crossed. Finally, they struggled up with their tongues hanging out but they had to wait for their eyes to get uncrossed again.

Seeing they were disabled for the moment by the wonder of his dancing, Brighton now gave up mere jumps and spins and began demonstrating his astonishing technique. Used as he was to dancing for animals, there was still a real challenge about touching the hearts of wolves. Besides, he knew he couldn't go on twirling and leaping high in the air all night. His very life depended on the quality of his dancing. He began with the first solo from *The Noble Savage*. Never in all his life, even at the School of Dramatic Art, had he been more graceful. First, he danced the loneliness of the Noble Savage, and the wolves (though they always travelled in a pack, and were never ever lonely) were so stirred that several of them pointed their noses into the air and howled in exact time to the music. It was most remarkable. Brighton now turned towards the wolves and began to express through dance his pleasure at seeing them. He made it very convincing. Some of the wolves began to wag their tails.

"He's really got something!" said the King of the Wolves. "This is high-class stuff." Of course, he said it in wolf language, but Brighton was good at reading the signs and became more poetic than ever before.

"Let me see," said the King of the Wolves, fascinated. "With a bit of practice I could manage an act like this myself. I always knew there was more to life than mere ravening. Come on! Let's give it a go!" The wolves began to point their paws and copy whatever movements Brighton made.

Seeing what they were about, Brighton began to encourage them by doing a very simple step and shouting instructions.

"You put your left paw in, you put your left paw out . . ."

Of course, the wolves could not understand the words, but Brighton was very clever at mime and they caught on to the idea of things, dancing with great enthusiasm. Naturally, they were not as graceful as Brighton, but then they had not practised for years as he had. Brighton could not help but be proud of them as they began a slow progress down the road back to the city, away from the forest and the sheep on the other side. The moon rose higher in the sky, and still Brighton danced, and the entranced wolves followed him pointing their paws. It was very late at night when they entered the city once more. People going home from the cinema stared and shouted, and pointed (fingers not toes). A lot of them joined in, either dancing or making music on musical instruments — banjos, trombones, combs — or anything that happened to be lying around.

In the School of Dramatic Art, wicked Antoine was just

about to dance the very part Brighton usually danced when the sound of the procession made him hesitate. The audience, full of curiosity, left the theatre. Outside was Brighton, swaying with weariness but still dancing, followed by twenty wolves, all dancing most beautifully by now, all in time and all very pleased with themselves, though, it must be admitted, all very hungry.

"Oh," cried the director of the School of Dramatic Art, rushing out to kiss Brighton on both cheeks. "What talent! What style! This will save the School of Dramatic Art from extinction."

"Send out for a supply of sausages," panted Brighton, "and write into the wolves' contracts that they will have not only sausages of the best quality, but that their names will appear in lights on top of the theatre. After all, if they are dancing here every night, they won't be able to chase and worry sheep, will they?"

After this, there was peace for a long time, both in the city and out on the farms (where the sheep grew very fat and woolly). The School of Dramatic Art did wonderfully well. People came from miles around to see Brighton and his dancing wolves, and, of course — just as he had predicted — after dancing until late at night, the wolves were too weary to go out ravening sheep. Everyone was delighted (except for the jealous dancers who just sulked and sizzled). Antoine, in particular, had such bad attacks of jealousy that it ruined his digestion and made his stomach rumble loudly, which forced him to abandon ballet altogether. However, Brighton, the wolves, the farmers, the director, and many other people, lived happily ever after in Hookywalker, that great city which people sometimes see looming out of the mist on the fringe of many fairy stories.

The Magician in the Tower

On the edge of the wood, in the soft and flickering shadows of the leaves, Matilda laughed and sighed as she said goodbye to her lover.

"We'll dream of each other tonight," she told him.

"And meet again tomorrow," he said. "But don't be late."

"Never, never, never!" cried Matilda, laughing.

They kissed each other; he went his way and she went hers. Because she was in love, Matilda felt herself powerful and happy — able to change the world with her smallest wish — so it gave her no surprise to come upon flowers, clumps of primroses and a cloud of forget-me-nots, breaking up the shadows under a bare tree. She thought that, by being so happy, she had invented a new season, a Matilda-season, fitting in somewhere between winter and spring, sharing a bit of both but different from either. The primroses and forget-me-nots were hers because, by being happy, she had made the air warm and the ground soft for them. So she picked herself a bunch of flowers, wrapped their stems in a dockleaf and went on her way home. However, to get home she had to pass the Magician's Tower.

There had always been a magician in the tower. The people in the town said, "The tower was there before our houses, before our village, and the magician has always lived in it. He must be an old, cobwebby fellow by now — very, very old." Their faces grew still for a moment as they thought just how old the magician must be. His tower was covered with a thousand years of climbing roses and ivy. Long windows, slots of darkness or light, showed through the thorns and leaves high on the wall. Sometimes, at night, these windows seemed to reflect sunlight from within; sometimes at midday, looking upwards and inwards, one could see what looked like stars. Sometimes the magician's shadow flickered like a mad giant, stretching out over fields and streams towards the hills, glimpsed for a moment and vanishing again. The magician himself was never seen and the door of his tower was never open.

However, tonight, as Matilda went by, she saw that her own enchanted Matilda-season had done more than open the primroses and forget-me-nots early, for the door of the Magician's Tower was open, too.

For a moment she stood staring. Walking away from a door open for the very first time ever seemed like turning your back on an invitation someone was offering you. From where she stood she could see the first two steps of a stair. Somewhere up the stair must be the magician himself, and Matilda suddenly felt sorry for him, an old man with only his mysteriousness to keep him company.

Feeling brave because she was in love and had invented a special new season, Matilda thought she might go up that staircase and give the magician her flowers. They would be a message of kindness from the world outside the tower where enchantment came about without the help of wizards and magicians. At the doorway she looked up and, under the dark, straggling fringe of leaves that covered the lintel, she could see letters cut into the stone, cut so deeply that, though worn with age, they were still clear. "The Tower of Changes" they said. But Matilda thought they must be wrong, for the tower was the most unchanged and unchanging thing she could imagine.

She stepped in through the open door. Suppose it shut behind her! But it didn't. She could still look back to the winter fields and the red, western, winter sun.

On the wall beside the third step was a picture in a dark frame of a smiling boy standing under an apple tree. Over his shoulder you could see a whole world — oceans and islands, hills, forests and cities. He was dressed in green with red curls falling to his collar and dark eyes that looked straight into Matilda's blue ones as if he were warning her of something and promising her another thing at one and the same time. Still and stiff in his paint, he held out towards her a bunch of primroses and forget-me-nots that seemed a reflection of her own, and his smile, like his eyes, promised and warned her. With astonishment Matilda saw that, though *he* was still, the landscape behind him was continually changing. A sun, as red as the sun outside the tower, rose up beyond the hills, climbed the blue air, and then turned into an apple upon the apple tree. A long, silver fish leaped from a stream that flowed past the boy's feet but, instead of falling back into the water, it flew on up into the sky and became a new moon. Tiny flowers opened in the grass, put out wings and changed to butterflies. A white flower with a golden heart and streaks of scarlet on its lower petals fell from a bush, and then a little white serpent with scarlet eyes and a gold key in its mouth slid off into the grass.

Further back, beyond boy and tree and stream and grass, the world of the picture moved and changed. Cities fell into ruin and were built again, waterfalls hesitated and then tumbled upwards, islands in the distant sea stretched themselves out into spiky green dragons and flew off into the stormy west. Among the flying up and the tumbling down the boy held out his flowers to Matilda as if offering to exchange them for those she held in her own hand.

Matilda smiled back at him and began to climb the stairs. Upwards, and upwards again, they led her and, at each turn in the spiral, there hung a picture. Strange faces passed before her eyes: one face as dark as a storm, eyes flashing lightning under thundering waves of black hair; one as clear as water, eyes like blue pools, hair as green as water cress; a third was a golden mask with holes for eyes, stalks of corn lying lightly between its smiling lips. Faces of bone, of feathers, of carved wood; an accidental face made of berries, stems and leaves that vanished when you looked at it directly... All these painted people watched Matilda climb the staircase and she, in turn, looked up at them through the friendly, careless tangle of her brown hair, holding the bunch of flowers in her scratched, strong little hands.

At last the stair ended, though the room at the top was more of a cave than a room, its walls of rough, unpolished rock, shining with long streaks of unknown minerals. A fire burned against the cave wall and Matilda's step on the stair echoed as if she had suddenly come into a space much greater than any space even the tower could hold.

The magician stood before her, painting a picture by the light of many candles crowded together on to rocks and ledges. His long, red and grey hair fell down his back almost to his waist. He turned and looked at her when he heard her step. He was not old, but, like Matilda, he had made a season of his own around him, and it was colder and darker than winter. Matilda found she could not speak to him. She merely held out her flowers and, rather than look at him, she looked past him at the picture he was painting. A blue-eyed woman in a blue dress was braiding her long, brown hair. Something shone in the candlelight. A tear, like a glassy beetle on a smooth golden leaf, was creeping down the woman's cheek. Putting her flowers down on a pile of old books, Matilda fled for, of all the paintings, this one frightened her most. Down the stairs and through the open door she ran and then stopped, astonished to find tears on her own cheek. She could not have said why she was crying.

Outside, nothing had changed. The world seemed exceptionally clear and understandable, its edges sure, its shapes continuous. As Matilda ran home the Magician's Tower was left behind. Her memories of it grew fainter, nor did she dream of it at night. By morning she was happy again, happy enough to feel ashamed of her flight the night before.

"There's no point in taking flowers to a known magician and then running away because you happen to see something magical. I shall go back and speak to him. He isn't old ... just sad and strange," she said to herself.

So that evening Matilda found herself once again at the Magician's Tower, and once again the door was open. Quickly, before she could be overcome by the strangeness of the tower, Matilda ran up the stairs, looking away from the faces that looked down at her, up and up, watching her own climbing feet until she entered the magician's room again. The cave had gone. Instead, the magician sat in a forest of ancient trees. His books lay on a rustling, crisp carpet of fallen leaves and he himself was less man than bird, covered in feathers which were crimson over his heart, golden on his cheeks and around his dark eyes, and red and grey over his head and down his back. The forest seemed to retreat beyond the possible boundaries of the tower, and the silence went deeper still. The painting stood on its big easel, but there were no paints and no brushes, for the magician was now working with the colours of his visions.

Matilda spoke quickly before she had time to become afraid.

"I'm sorry I ran away yesterday," she said. "I hope you liked my flowers."

The magician remained silent, pointing to his picture. The blue-eyed brown-haired woman was now holding the bundle of primroses and forget-me-nots. Each flower shone with a light of its own – no longer a simple sign of spring, but full of a different, darker promise – beautiful but menacing.

The magician gestured towards the flowers again as if to say, "Look closely", and Matilda walked over to stare deep into the heart of the picture's flowers. Through the paint they showed their truth to her, their hard struggle under the earth, their rise to power in the spring.

The magician offered her a wooden cup filled with water. As he held it out, Matilda noticed the back of his hand was covered with little blue and green feathers. Those below his fingernails were as small as marigold seeds. The water tasted of leaves. The berries he gave her were sweet and sharp. Matilda smiled and thanked him and, though he did not smile back, she imagined she saw kindness in his eyes. He did not speak either but, when a moment later she went down the stair, a strange cry, a cool cry, both soft and harsh, came after her, and she knew that the magician had cried out to her in the voice of a fabulous bird.

'He's enchanted. He's stopped being a human being,' Matilda thought. 'Perhaps if I bring him a present he'll become a person again, like Prince Frog.'

Now, when she walked past a clump of crocuses they seemed to have changed in some way. No longer were they just pretty flowers, but a force of spears cutting through the dark and cold — beautiful and ruthless spirits driving winter before them.

The following day, Matilda came to the Magician's Tower for the third time, and found there was no cave at the top of the stairs and no forest of ancient trees, either. Instead, there was a wide plain stretching as far as she could see. As the wind swept over it, billowing grasses reflected the light in shifting waves, and it seemed to Matilda that the wind was writing a huge message over the plain, a message she might read herself if only she were cleverer. Then something moved far away. She forgot the scribbling wind and looked up to see what was coming towards her. Herds of galloping horses, red, white and black, shook the ground as they came nearer and nearer.

For a moment, Matilda imagined she was going to be trodden into the grass. But they wheeled and reared before her and then began feeding peacefully, all except for the leader of the herd who stood over her, his red and grey mane blowing against her face. She smiled with relief to see his eyes were the eyes of the magician.

"Oh, it's you," she said. "I've brought you a present. A loaf of bread which I made myself. Do you eat bread when you are a horse?" The horse began to change its shape, shifting so swiftly that she couldn't quite see what was happening until he stood before her, almost a man but a man with a mane growing down his neck and back, a man with the ears of a horse.

"Thank you for the bread," he said, and those were the first words she heard him speak, talking in the voice of a rusty key turned in an old lock. "It is a long time since I had a present — and now I have had two within a week."

"I don't count the flowers," Matilda said.

"I do," said the magician.

Matilda started going to the tower every day, and every day she took something with her — an empty snailshell, a hawk's feather, a nutshell filled with mosses and tiny ferns. At the top of the stair she might find a seashore, a desert, a mountain top, or fields of snow and ice, but the magician was always there, and whatever she brought him he took and changed for her. Bread was never the same for her after she had given some to the magician. Cutting a slice, she would feel the slow growth of the wheat, the ripening of the grain, the rain that had fallen on it, the sun that had shone. She herself became the bread, living for a little in it

like a good spirit under the arch of its crust.

"For goodness sake, Matilda!" cried her mother. "You're a proper dreamer these days. The sooner you're married, the better, that's all I can say. You take a day to cut a slice of bread!"

Matilda blinked, thinking that she had lived in the bread for what seemed a hundred years.

One day, the magician, shining in silver scales, half fish, half dragon, gave her a book to look at. The first few pages were covered in drawings, but then words took over — many languages in many different sorts of writing. There was no title page.

"This is the book of the magicians of the tower," he told her. "This is *The Book of Changes.*"

On the first page there was a wise, cool face drawn in charcoal, eyes cast down, a smile at the corners of its mouth. Suddenly the eyes looked up out of the page as if they recognized Matilda, lips opened as if to speak. Before any words were spoken, however, the face darkened and changed and then changed again so that from the same page many faces looked rapidly out at her — faces black as storm, bright as day, old and young, smiling, glaring, laughing, weeping. At the very last she thought she recognized first one face and then, perhaps, another, but before she could be sure, the first face returned again, with its eyes shut and its mouth stern, a face refusing to tell. Matilda looked at the magician shyly.

"I thought I saw your face for a moment," she said. She could not talk about the other faces that she might have recognized.

"Those are the faces of the magicians of the tower," the magician answered. "There were others before me."

"I thought you had been here always," Matilda cried. "There has always been a magician in the tower."

"I am not one but many," the magician told her. "Others have been before me and there will be others after me."

Matilda frowned. "But why?" she asked at last. "What *do* you do here – you magicians?"

"We think about the world," the magician said, "and after a while we become the world, as you have seen. We go into birds and mud, and into horses, thistles and fireflies. We become stones and cobwebs, and waves in the sea. We are born over and over again and we rot. Without the dreams of the magicians perhaps the world would become thin and uncertain. Perhaps the world you see is held together by our dreams. Perhaps, without us, birds would leave their trees to swim in the sea, babies would be born with tails and manes of lions, and witches, who feed on disorder, would take over everything. The magicians hold the patterns of the world together. Their lives are like stitches in patchwork."

"I hope that visitors don't put you off, then," Matilda said, laughing a little. "You talk more than you used to, Mr Magician. Don't forget your dreaming."

The magician gave her a look, both kind and sad, which for some reason terrified her, and she left the tower thinking, I don't need to go back again. I'll never go back.

But she came back the next day and began to read *The Book of Changes* where it lay open upon the bank of an angry river. She read until a bunch of decaying reeds became a swirling mist and then, gradually, a man. From then on, though the magician became better at talking, Matilda became better at silence. Her silences led her to feel like the seed in the ground. She, too, broke open to release the white downward bending root and the pale, upward turning shoot. She too held up first, blind leaves like hands. She became the tiny egg, the creeping, greedy caterpillar, the jewelled chrysalis and the butterfly. Coming out of a dream of birds she was alarmed to find her hands covered in tiny feathers, as soft and brown as her hair. But, as she stared, they melted and ran down her fingers, like drops of water from a stream.

In the world outside the tower, people noticed Matilda changing.

"Matilda — what's got into you?" cried her mother, anxiously. "Don't just stand there staring at the sky. There's nothing up there to see. Not even a cloud! Not even a bird!"

"I'm looking at the stars," Matilda heard her own voice say, sounding like a voice faintly heard from another far-off room.

"There aren't any stars," her mother replied desperately. "It's broad daylight." And so it was, but Matilda could see the stars spread like grains of salt spilt across the afternoon sky.

"You've changed," said her lover. "You don't listen to me any more. I scarcely ever see you. Where are you every afternoon? Why do you plait your hair now? I liked it loose."

"To keep it out of my eyes," Matilda stammered. "Out of my eyes while I'm reading." She tried to listen to his voice, but the voices of the trees filled her ears — some drowsy with winter, some stormy and leaping with the new spring. She tried to see his face clearly but the faces of the magicians, dark and fair, flickered before her, dazzling her with sunlight and shadow. People around her began to flash and fade like moths dying in a candle flame. In the world outside the tower things began to change before her very eyes. Bare trees blossomed, broke into leaf, swelled with green fruit. The fruit ripened and fell, the leaves turned golden and, falling too, sank into the ground like water, leaving the tree bare once more.

I mustn't go to the tower again, Matilda thought.

But *The Book of Changes* had laid its enchantment on her. Later that day she looked up from reading the book to find the magician offering her wild strawberries, and she couldn't tell whether she had been reading, looking at pictures, or living in the print on the page. The book talked of secret rocks that no man saw melting and seething in the heart of the world, of tiny mosses that lived and died undiscovered, of fish swimming in the black heart of the sea, lit only by their own luminous sides, of the forces clenching atoms together, or wrenching them apart. Everything changed, said the book. Men and plants and animals were born and died and crumbled in magical decay, mountains wore away, the moon grew cold, the stars fell in on themselves and were crushed into nothingness. "Everything changes," sang the voices in her ears. "You are changing. You are changing."

Now the tower was the only place where things stood still for Matilda. Her parents, her lover, were like puppets in a play that was being acted both forwards and backwards at the same time. She did not always know if she were seeing them today, yesterday or tomorrow. But the magician did not change. In the tower the stones stayed still and the pictures no longer moved as she walked past them.

One day Matilda woke up and opened her eyes, not on the walls of her room but on a grove of trees. Putting on her blue dress the trees were felled and cut into timber. As she combed her hair the walls of the house rose about her and for a moment she stood in her safe, familiar room. But as she braided her hair the house tumbled at some moment in the future, and grasses like lean flames rose up through cracks in the boards. Reflected in her looking glass she saw, not her own face, but a desert of ice and snow, lit with a lurid light reflected from the looking-glass sky that was hung with curtains of fire.

Like someone blinded, she groped her way where she had once run, over a familiar road that she glimpsed briefly before it burst into a wilderness of weeds and blackberries and then vanished entirely. Somehow she reached the tower and fell through that terrible, open door. She sat on the bottom step with her eyes closed, while behind her lids the world still whirled and swayed, offering everything of itself at once.

When she opened her eyes at last she saw the picture of the boy in green offering his primroses and forget-me-nots. Matilda sighed and stood up wearily. Then she walked up the stairs. The room at the top of the stairs was a room with walls and bookcases and windows looking out over the countryside. The magician stood beside a large, old desk, straightening some papers. He wore green velvet, his hair had been cut and red curls now hung down to his collar.

"Oh," said Matilda, seeing something for the first time. "You are the boy in the painting at the bottom of the stairs."

"Yes," said the magician, "and look there." He pointed

to a painting on a wooden stand. There was the painting of the woman with the braided, brown hair and the blue dress, the painting she had seen when she first visited the tower. There was the reflection which her looking glass had refused to reveal that morning.

"It's me," Matilda said. "You were painting my picture when I brought you the flowers."

"No," he replied. "I was painting the picture of the next magician."

"I don't want to be the magician!" Matilda cried desperately, but he shook his head.

"That's what we all say," he answered.

"Why did you choose me?" she cried again.

"I didn't choose you, though I saw you coming towards me," the magician replied. "It's always the world that chooses its magicians. It sent you the flowers and it opened the door of the tower. It always knew what you were — where you would be. And believe me, Matilda, there is no place for you now outside the tower. The magicians who refuse the tower go mad out there. Seasons riot; the people they love are born, grow old and fall to dust a thousand times a day; the hands of the clocks spin like windmills. Here, at least, you'll be able to understand something. Think bird and be bird. Think grass and be grass. Be fish, be moth, be star, be stone. As you live in these things, the world will hold still outside the tower for your mother, your father — your lover, too."

"What will they think now I'm gone? They'll miss me. I know they'll miss me."

"They will miss you but in the end they'll forget you. People don't remember for ever," the magician told her. "And now the time has come when I must go too, for *you*

105

are the new magician and I must move one place on."

"What's your next role?" Matilda asked, curiously.

"I won't know until I get there," the magician said. "I'll know soon. You, too, some day. One place further on!"

First, they hung her picture next to his at the bottom of the stairs.

"On my way!" he said, smiling. Then he stepped out of the door of the tower into the sunshine which dissolved him at once. Up he went like a mist drawn into the spring air. Then the door closed and could not be opened again.

Matilda climbed upstairs under the dark and light faces of the pictures, like the faces of night and day.

And she thought bird, and flew high in the sky. She thought stone, and lay like a silent heart in the breast of the world. She thought fire, and blazed in the core of the mountains. Outside the tower people wept for her and finally forgot her, but she thought leaf, trapping sunlight in her green cells. Storm and tempest raged around the tower like black lions, but she thought summer and became golden, for she truly was the magician of the tower and would be until some other person came with a handful of flowers to set her free. For there has always been a magician in the tower and there always will be.